Mortal Mate

VIOLA TEMPEST

Contents

1. Gemma — 1
2. Quentin — 9
3. Gemma — 15
4. Quentin — 25
5. Gemma — 29
6. Quentin — 35
7. Gemma — 47
8. Quentin — 55
9. Gemma — 69
10. Quentin — 73
11. Gemma — 79
12. Quentin — 87
13. Gemma — 95
14. Quentin — 103
15. Gemma — 111
16. Quentin — 121
Epilogue — 133

MORTAL MATE

VIOLA TEMPEST

CHAPTER 1
Gemma

I sit up in bed, gasping for breath. I run a hand along my face, blinking furiously until my eyes adjust to the darkness surrounding me.

It's the same dream that wakes me every night. It always starts okay, perfect even. I'm back in my childhood bedroom, sixteen years old and innocent to the world around me. Quentin Forsyth is there, my next-door neighbor and closest friend.

But then the dream shifts, taking me to the time when

the moving truck arrived, and he was whisked from my life completely. But lately, I've been having these dreams, where it's him... but older. He's the same age as me, but something else has changed as well. What happens next is always different, but somehow, the dream always twists. And suddenly, it's not Quentin, but rather a monster wearing his face.

I swing my legs over on the bed. I already know that trying to get back to sleep would be futile. Grabbing my phone from off the side table, I see that it's still hours before my shift starts, but I can at least get a head start on the day.

It doesn't take long for me to shower and get dressed. By the time I sit down at the dining table with my cup of coffee, my roommate is only just getting out of bed.

"Morning," Micaela says with a yawn, pulling her robe tightly around herself. "God, Gemma, what time did you wake up this morning?"

She pours herself a cup of coffee from the pot I made and sits down across from me. She's never been an early bird, and her heavily lidded eyes struggle to stay open. Even half-asleep, she still looks good. I've always questioned how she can always be flawlessly beautiful without trying.

"Early," I respond flatly.

"Do you have work today?" she asks when she figures out that I'm not going to give her previous question further explanation.

"Yeah." I take a sip from my mug and place it down onto the solid wooden table. "It's just a noon shift, though."

"Are we still on for tonight?" Micaela asks.

I raise an eyebrow. "Tonight?" I don't think I've forgotten anything.

Micaela gasps, slapping my shoulder. "You promised last week that we'd go to the club! You know, that one on Baker Street that everyone's been raving about for forever."

I take a deep breath and lean my head back. "Did I?"

"Gemma!"

"Okay, okay," I say, raising my hands into the air and chuckling. "I'll come home after work, shower, and we can go for a while. I'm not staying out all night, though."

She smirks. "That's what you say every time we go out."

"Oh, shut up," I remark, but I laugh.

There's silence for a while as I sip the rest of my coffee. My mind drifts back to the dream I had last night. Quentin's smile haunts my mind, even though I know he's gone. He left years ago, and he's never coming back.

"You're thinking about him again, aren't you?" Micaela asks, and my eyes snap up to meet hers. "Quentin. I know that look on your face."

"I don't know what you're talking about," I say, standing from the table and wandering over to the sink. I rinse out my cup and place it onto the counter.

"Gemma," Micaela moans reproachfully. "Talk to me."

"I had another dream," I tell her. "They're becoming more frequent again."

She's quiet for a few minutes, and I turn to look at her. Her face is drawn up in thought. I can see she's hesitating to tell me something.

"What?" I demand. "You think I'm going insane?"

The question was meant to be rhetorical, but Micaela hums to herself. "Not insane. I just think you're spending way too much time thinking about your past. I know your father—"

"Don't bring my father into this," I snap. I don't mean it to come out as harsh as it does.

"You have to forget about Quentin. All this worrying isn't going to get you anywhere."

"And how do you suppose I get him out of my head?" My temper escalates, and my face flushes with heat. "Just forgetting about it doesn't exactly help, Micaela."

She shrugs, completely nonchalant. "If you're going to yell at me, I don't want to hear it. All I'm saying is that you need to figure out why you're so hung up on a boy you lost eleven years ago." I don't have any words for this, but luckily, Micaela has never had any issues with speaking her mind. "I think you deserve a night out. Let loose; forget about the past."

"Easier said than done," I mutter. "I'm going to get ready. Let me know when Jayden gets here."

I spend the rest of the morning getting ready for work. I pack my bag with my uniform: a skimpy outfit that I could never wear in public and a sparkly headband to match. I pack some granola bars, and shove some sports drinks in as an afterthought. Once I'm confident I have everything I'll need, I sit on our couch and flip through some of the channels on the television.

A familiar buzz sounds from a panel in the wall, and my head snaps around. Micaela beats me to it, and responds by pressing a button to allow the person in. "It's him," she tells me. "I think it's so sweet that he drives you to work every day."

"Well, he's working from home right now, and he doesn't really like me using public transportation. Says I'm too good for it." I shrug. The sentiment is nice, but I hate having to rely on someone this much. I'd much rather take the bus and pay the extra fare.

Micaela makes a sound in the back of her throat to indicate something, like delight or tenderness. "I wish I have someone like that."

I take a deep breath. "Yeah."

"You should invite him out with us tonight!"

I stiffen. "Uhm, no. It's really not his crowd. He's never really been into the 'normal' definition of a fun night out."

"Boring," Micaela says, elongating the first syllable. She yawns dramatically, causing me to roll my eyes.

Before long, there's a knock on the front door, and I swing it open to reveal a tall, lanky figure. Jayden stands there, hands shoved inside his pockets.

"Hey, Gemma," he says, leaning forward to peck me on the cheek.

"Hey," I echo, then turn to Micaela. "I'll see you after my shift, okay?"

She sends me a mock-salute, and I step out into the hall, closing the door behind myself. Until it's just Jayden and I, both of us awkwardly waiting for the other to say something first.

I crack. "Shall we?"

He nods, and I start down the hallway toward the elevator. We've been dating for about a year now, ever since we matched on an online dating app during a personal moment of weakness. And since then, he's been a solid rock to lean on and remind me that good people still exist.

"I'm having dinner with my family tomorrow. You're welcome to come, if you'd like."

A grin spreads across my face. I've always loved his

parents and sister like they're my own, and the feeling is reciprocated. "Sure. You'll come pick me up?"

"Of course," he says, matching my grin. "My mom misses you coming over to bake cookies with her."

I almost cringe at the thought. "I didn't think she wanted me back since I almost burned down your kitchen last time."

He chuckles. "No harm done."

"Then I'll set something up with her," I say, nodding my head. His mom is the loveliest, most pure-hearted woman on the planet. She reminds me of the few memories I have of my own mother before she passed away. It's nice having that figure back in my life.

"Good. Dad won't say it, but he misses gorging himself on baked goods every weekend."

I don't say anything, but simply smile. Jayden's father is just as kind as his wife, and the complete opposite of my own paternal figure.

I honestly don't know what I'd do without all of them.

"BYE, HAVE A GOOD DAY," JAYDEN TELLS ME, leaning across the console in his car to peck my lips. "I'll come pick you up at five?"

"Five-thirty," I correct. "And thank you again; you seriously don't have to drive me everywhere, you know."

"I know," he says, and kisses me again. "I'll see you later."

I step out of the car, my backpack clutched in my hand. I wave as he drives away, and don't move until he's left the parking lot and out of sight completely. I spare a glance up at the restaurant sign above the door. I've been to Macey's Bar and Grill a few times, but never with Jayden or Micaela. I always tell them that, after working there for so long, I can't stomach going there in my spare time.

In reality, I've never even submitted an application to Macey's. They're never hiring, anyway.

I shoulder my backpack and turn to walk down the street. Not too far down the road is Baker Street, which I turn down and walk a little way to Temptation; the *adult entertainment club* as it's more respectfully known as. During the day, it operates more as a bar and lunch spot with dancers to appease the male audience. At night, it gets more tip-heavy, but all the girls want *those* spots. Better routines and a larger crowd mean more money, and the night goes by faster.

After pushing open the front doors, I make my way into the back. It's a tight, close-knit area lined with vanities across one wall and racks of costumes along another. Curtains wall off changing rooms, but hardly anyone bothers with them.

"Gemma!" One of my favorite coworkers, Shelly, calls out. "Stuck with the early shift, huh? Well, at least we don't have to deal with the insanity of tonight."

"What's so special about tonight?" I ask, shedding off my boots and pulling my outfit from my bag. "It's just another Friday night."

Shelly smiles. "You didn't hear? Apparently, they're doing another event. 'Blacklist,' I think they're calling it. It's some sort of 'take three shots, get a fourth one free' type of deal. It's going to be crazy full of drunks."

I cringe and run a hand down my face. "Don't tell me that. I've got to come here later with my roommate."

Shelly tilts her head to the side. "Does she know you work here?"

I shake my head. "Not if I can help it."

"You know the drill. Write it on the mirror," she says, jutting her chin toward the large, floor-to-ceiling mirror that covers nearly the entire wall.

Hanging in a basket and screwed into the wall is a cup of dry-erase markers that are used to write down schedules, notes to each other, and positive messages. One of the corners is written "classified," with a list of girls' names underneath. If a coworkers' name is on that list, it means we have to pretend we've never met them before at any cost. I grab one of the blue markers and scribble my name down onto the mirror.

I have a feeling it's going to be a long, long night.

CHAPTER 2
Quentin

I'm sixteen. The entire house is quiet beyond the whirr of the fan circulating air through my bedroom. I shuffle forward on my bed to sit at the edge. My room is plain; everything is mostly gray or white. I had little say in the decorating. However, things I do have control over are the posters up on my walls. Different classic vampires from movies, comics, and a variety of different mediums hang on the wall with thumb tacks. My mother isn't happy about it, but reluctantly understands my obsession.

My window is open, and through it, I can see a girl. She's small, petite, and sits hunched at her desk, scribbling away at the homework I know I should also be doing. Her long blonde hair is draped over her shoulders haphazardly, but I think it's adorable. She's still in her workout clothes, and I know from prior conversations that she's just come home from javelin practice.

I stare for longer than what's acceptable. We've been friends ever since we were children, but as soon as high school came along, we became distanced, though no fault of hers. We've stayed friendly, but I've always had the biggest crush on her.

Supposedly sensing my stare, she looks up and twists in her chair. I raise my hand in a wave, smiling sheepishly. She waves back, a wide grin spreading over her face.

Making her way over to the window, she pulls open the glass and leans onto the sill. "Hey, Quentin." My heart leaps at how she says my name. "What did you think about Mrs. Delana's lesson today?"

I rub the back of my neck. "I wasn't paying attention." I was staring at you the entire time, is what I neglect to add.

She laughs, her shoulders shaking as she hangs her head. "You've got to take Algebra more seriously."

"I'll take that into consideration," I say, staring intently into her piercing blue orbs. She opens her mouth to say something, but is cut off by an angry voice.

"Gemma!" I hear her father's voice slur from somewhere inside her house. She flinches, her smile instantly dropping from her face.

She places her hands upon the sliding glass. "I'll see you tomorrow, okay?" Without waiting for a reply, she slams the window shut and pulls the curtains across, entirely blocking me out.

That's the last time I see her for a long, long time.

~

LATER THAT NIGHT, I SIT AT THE TABLE AND POKE around at the food on my plate. My mom has made tofu and steamed vegetables. I can barely stomach this new vegetarian diet she's forced upon all of us. I lock eyes with my father for a split second and see him slip a piece to the dog under the table. I avert my gaze and clear my throat.

"What's wrong, sweetie?" My mother asks. "You've barely touched your food."

"I'm just not very hungry," I tell her. In reality, I'm starving. But this stuff has never satisfied my appetite.

My mom sighs, her fork clinking against the plate as she sets it down. "Is this the vampire thing again?" When I don't answer, she turns to my father. "Owen, help me out here."

He coughs, his hand springing back onto the table as the dog munches happily on a carrot. My mom glares at him. "Quentin, eat what your mother made," he says finally, looking to his wife for confirmation. Hypocrite.

"I'm seriously not hungry," I say, pushing the plate away from myself. "Can I go up to my room?" My parents share a glance, and my eyes narrow at the sight.

My father takes a deep breath. "Look, Quentin. We were going to wait until later to tell you, but—"

"What's going on?" I demand, looking between them.

"Your father got a promotion, but it's in Wilburn. He starts on Monday."

I'm excited for a few moments before I realize something. "Wilburn is three counties away. He's going to drive there and back every day?"

My mother shakes her head. "We're moving first thing tomorrow morning. Movers will be packing up everything and bringing them along to the new house."

My head spins. "Are you serious?"

"Everything happened so quickly," my dad says. "I only found out this morning. We found a real estate agent who got a great deal on...," my father continues talking, but I don't hear anything beyond a faint ringing in my ears.

What about Gemma? I'm just supposed to... leave? "We can't just go," I plead. "I have friends; I have school. I can't even say goodbye?"

"We thought it was better this way," my mother says softly.

I stand up from the table, my chair scratching against the wood as I do. Without another word, I leave and head up to my room.

My hands ball into fists. How could they do this to me?

Looking out my window, I see that Gemma's own curtains are still drawn shut. I want, desperately, to see her, to tell her I'm leaving, and how I've felt about her all these years. But no matter how much I wish she would pull open the fabric and look out, she never does.

I grab a pencil off my desk and throw it across the gap between our houses. It taps pathetically against the glass and falls to the grass below.

"Gemma!" I call out, but it's no use. She must be down-

stairs or having dinner. Or perhaps, she doesn't even want to see me at all.

I try for another ten minutes until my cup of pencils and markers is completely emptied. I sit down on my bed and stare up at the poster on the ceiling. It's old and torn in some places, but it's signed by one of my favorite actors.

I shut my eyes, trying and failing to drown out the entire world.

~

RAIN POUNDS MERCILESSLY, DRENCHING ME FROM head to toe. It's been six years since the move, and I still hate this city with a passion. The only upside is that this city is easy to blend in, get lost inside the fray of all the other miserable citizens.

I round the corner, and despite the darkness and rain, I see a cloaked figure standing in my path.

"What the hell?" I demand and attempt to side-step the man. He simply mirrors my movement, gracefully blocking my path.

Temper boils in my veins. I don't have time for this.

But before I can do or say anything, searing hot pain shoots down my arm and through my entire body. It takes me a moment to realize that, in a split second, the man had grabbed my arm and brought my wrist to his mouth.

My back stiffens, and I cry out. The pain quickly turns into something else, something more.

I curse, but the man keeps holding my arm tight against his face. Eventually, he looks up at me, and I see pale white skin reflecting in the moonlight. My blood drips from his chin, and he smiles.

More excruciating pain, and I look down to see a handle sticking out between my ribs. A knife. I've just been stabbed with a knife.

My vision blurs, and the last thing I hear is the pale man laughing as I fall to the ground.

CHAPTER 3
Gemma

"**G**irl, you look *good*."

"Yeah?" I ask, twirling around in my short, black dress. In reality, it's more flattering than most of the outfits I wear to the club, but Micaela doesn't know that.

"Absolutely," she says. "Can you zip me up?"

I step over to help her with the back of her dress, zipping up the red material and folding down the metal tab so it doesn't come undone during the night.

"Micaela," I say, looking at our reflections. "We're smoking hot."

She chuckles and pushes my shoulder playfully. "I don't know where you pulled these dresses from, but I'm glad you found them. And thanks for letting me borrow your mascara!"

I gape at her. "*That's* where it went."

"Come on, we're going to be late," she sings. "I told Alex we'd be there by eleven."

"Hold on." I shuffle around the room, looking around and under my comforter. "I think my clutch is around here somewhere."

"What do you need it for? Just put your phone in your bra," she says, gesturing toward her own chest. "It's what I'm doing."

I raise an eyebrow and look between her and I. "Not everyone is graced with a rack like yours," I tell her with a laugh. "Unfortunately, I *do* need a clutch."

"I think I saw it out on the couch," she says with a fake defeated sigh, jabbing her thumb toward the door of my bedroom.

I shuffle down the hall and to the living room, where I find my black sparkly clutch. It has a wrist strap and is just large enough to hold some cash and my phone. It's been my partner for many nights out and hasn't let me down yet.

"What shoes are you wearing?" Micaela calls, still in my bedroom. "And can I borrow your silver ones?"

"Go for it," I respond, and grab my phone off the coffee table. When I do, I see an unopened message from Jayden from a few minutes ago on the screen. I punch in my passcode and read, "*We're going out to eat tomorrow. Dad forgot to pick up the roast. Does MaryAnn's Diner sound okay?"* I send him back a quick reply, assuring him that I'm good with whatever they decide to do. After all, a free meal is a free meal.

"Does my hair look okay?" Micaela asks, emerging down the hall. She plays with the curls, running her fingers through and bouncing them. "Or should I straighten it again?"

I shake my head. "No, I like the curls. Makes you look like a badass."

She smirks. "Thanks, Gem. Are you ready to go? The next bus leaves in five minutes."

"Yeah, just about," I tell her, throwing my phone into the clutch and making sure I have at least fifty dollars in bills.

The bus stop is luckily just around the corner from the apartment building. The air outside, although slightly crisp, is warm enough that we don't have to wear sweaters. It's evident that it has rained recently, as puddles line the streets, and everything is coated in a thin layer of moisture.

Sounds of cars and people chattering fill the air, and I'm barely able to hear when Micaela mutters, "I don't understand why we don't go out more often. This is so exciting!"

"We're not even there yet," I point out. "Keep your comments reined in until tomorrow when you're hungover with your head in a toilet."

She sticks her tongue out at me, but the bus has arrived, so she's saved from my retort. We both climb aboard the surprisingly packed transit, picking spots to stand near the front. It almost startles me how crowded it is, but then I remember that it's a Friday night, and I'm used to being chauffeured around by my boyfriend.

Eventually, we make it to the club. I feign never having been here before, making statements such as, "are you sure this is the right place" and "it's certainly well-decorated."

The place is packed, more so than I've seen it in a long time. The lights, as always, are dimmed. Neon fluorescents line the bar and stages, where some of my coworkers are dancing.

"You want a drink?" I shout to Micaela, who is standing on her tiptoes and scanning the crowd.

"Sure, I'll have anything sweet," she says back, not looking at me but rather locking eyes with various strangers before moving on to the next..

I head off toward the bar, which is being manned by the manager's son and his new apprentice. Kyle is tall, skinny, and has hit on me many times in the past. I've yet to be introduced to the trainee.

"Hey, Gemma!" Kyle shouts. I place a finger to my lips and shake my head vigorously. "Ah, shoot. Sorry."

"It's alright," I tell him. "Can I get two margaritas? And can you make one with a few shots of simple syrup?"

"Sure thing," he says, dipping below the counter to grab various ingredients. I take the time to look around, surveying the kind of people who are here tonight.

"Seems like a nice crowd," I tell Kyle. "Tell me more about this 'Blacklist' thing."

"Every fourth shot is on the house," he tells me while he pours the concoction into two martini glasses. He adds a lemon wedge to both, and then to Micaela's, he puts an additional lemon twist. "Enjoy your night!"

I nod, and take a sip from my glass as I hunt my friend back down. She's notorious for wandering off, but I'm determined to keep an eye on her tonight. With this event, she's bound to do something stupid.

"You found Alex!" I exclaim when I finally make my way over to Micaela. The two are dancing together, and my roommate's boyfriend already has a drink in his hand. From a glance, it looks like whiskey. I hand Micaela her drink, ensuring she has a firm grip before letting go.

"How long have you been here for?" I ask the redhead currently grinding on my friend.

"About half an hour," he says, standing up straight and wrapping his arms around me. "Good to see you again!"

"You have to come over to our place more often," I tell him. "Micaela doesn't shut up when you're gone." She blushes and coughs, taking a sip of her drink for something to do.

"Let's get this party started!" Alex says, raising his drink into the air.

FOUR MARGARITAS AND SEVEN SHOTS IN, I'M starting to forget why, exactly, it's been so long since I've been out to the club.

"Where's my free one, Kyle?!" I shout above all the noise, slamming my empty shot glass onto the table. "I don't care what it is; just give me something," I hiccup, "good."

"Everything here is good," he says in an annoyingly sober voice. Why would anyone ever want to be sober?

"You should have a glass of water before downing anything else."

"You're not my dad," I tell him. "Well... I doubt even my own dad would try and stop me. Who knows? Maybe he'd hit me over it."

It takes him a few moments to answer. "Your dad's abusive?"

I shake my head. "Who told you that?"

"Gemma, I swear. Drink this glass of water, and I'll give you the shot. Okay?"

I glare at the glass. It looks so deceptively like vodka, but it's not. I know it's not.

"What if you and Micaela race?" He suggests, and it's then I realize that my best friend has shown up at the bar next to me.

"Only if you and Alex race, too," I tell him. "Come on, are you scared that a little *girl* will beat you?" I taunt, picking up the glass of water and waving it in the air. A few drops splash out of the cup, but not enough to give me any sort of advantage.

"Alright," Kyle says, bringing out three more glasses and putting water into them, "On three."

"One," I say, holding my glass and staring intently at the sloshing liquid. It can't be *that* bad. "Two." Okay, maybe it's going to be pretty bad. How does something not have any smell? "Three."

It's bland and tastes so much like nothing that I almost spit it out. Somehow, I manage to swallow everything in the glass, hardly getting anything on my face. I slam the cup onto the bar, cheering.

"I beat all of you," I brag, pointing at each of them in turn. "I'm the drinking queen!"

While I turn around to do my happy dance, I spot something in the corner of my eye. I stop, staring intently until my eyes manage to focus on an individual on the other side of the room.

Quentin. It's him, and I know it. He looks exactly like the older version in my dreams, and now he's here, watching me at the club. I rub my eyes with my fingers in an attempt to clear away some of the haziness, but when I pull my hands away, he's gone.

I frantically scan the room, looking for anywhere he could have gone. How could he have left so suddenly? I only had my eyes closed for a moment.

Maybe my mind was playing tricks on me. Perhaps Kyle is right, and I *don't* need that eighth shot. As if I called it upon myself, my stomach churns, and the room spins faster and faster, leaving me behind. I start swaying on my feet.

"Gemma, are you alright?" It's Micaela, her hand on my shoulder and looking down at me with concern.

"I don't feel too good," I tell Micaela. "I'm going to get some air."

Her eyes widen with concern despite her own drunken state. "Do you want me to come with you?"

I shake my head. "I'll be alright. I have my phone on me."

"I'm coming with you," Alex tells me, putting his glass down onto the bar.

"No," I say, placing a hand on his chest. "Keep an eye on Micaela. I'm not sure she can hold down her liquor as well as I can."

I head over to the area where I swear I saw Quentin, but he's no longer there. I ask a few people if they've seen a tall, brooding figure, but nobody has. Perhaps I did imagine the entire thing.

The world spins harder, and I feel like I'm going to be sick. I head over to the employee's only section, pushing past the swinging doors and bolting down the corridor.

The exit door to the alley is one I've used hundreds of times. It's a common space for dancers to get away or take a breath after being trapped in a hot room for hours on end. I prop open the heavy door with a loose brick so it doesn't close and lock behind me.

I lean against the gray wall and take a deep breath, gulping down oxygen and wishing the world would just stop spinning. My heart pounds faster than ever. Why did I ever think this was a good idea?

Thoughts of Quentin find their way into my brain. I could have sworn that it was him inside, staring at me from across the crowd of people. But maybe I'm just too hot or too drunk, or a combination of both. Maybe my brain was seeing what I wanted to be real instead of what was.

Quentin is gone. He's never coming back.

"Hey, pretty thing," a voice slurs from somewhere down the alley. When I glance up and around, a large figure has made its way over to me. Before I can react, they kick the brick from the threshold and push the door closed. My heart pounds harder, but now for a completely different reason. The only other way back into the club is on the other side of the building, and I'm sure my legs wouldn't be able to carry me nearly fast or far enough to reach it.

"You're hot. Have I seen you before?"

I chew on the inside of my cheek. Keeping my voice steady, I say, "You must have me confused with someone else. I can help you find them if you'd like."

"No, no," he says, his eyes squinting and tapping his finger on his lips. Then his eyes widen with realization. "You're that dancer from this morning! You work here."

I cross my arms over my chest, trying to cover up as much exposed skin as I can. Still, his eyes trail over me, making my skin crawl. "Nope, I'm just waiting for a friend. She said she'd be meeting me here in a few minutes."

"I think you're lying to get me to go away. Are you lying to me, sweet cheeks?"

"I never lie," I tell him. I'm surprised with how steady my voice sounds despite being drunk and terrified. My fingers twitch, and I remember my phone that's in the clutch attached to my wrist. Taking it out would draw too much attention, especially since I can barely see straight, and any attempt I make would be clumsy and uncoordinated.

"Then she can join. I'm not opposed to a threesome."

"Well, *I* am," I tell him. In my experience, it's always better to be direct with these types of guys. Direct — but not aggressive. But this man is either too stupid or too intoxicated to understand what I'm saying.

He reaches out his groping hands, placing them onto my hips. I go for my phone, but he grabs my wrists and holds them against the wall with surprising strength.

"You're hurting me," I tell him. "Get off, *get off*."

"I think you like it," he boasts, his hot, vodka-smelling breath filling my nostrils. I fight the urge to gag. "I think, with an outfit like that, you're practically begging—"

Before he can finish, he's suddenly thrown backwards and into the dumpster across the alley. I gasp, looking around for any indication of what just happened. A black-hooded figure rushes over to the greasy man now sprawled out across the concrete ground.

"No!" the man pleads, but the cloaked man doesn't hesitate. He punches him, once. Twice. The pervert sobs, feebly attempting to block his face with his arms.

"Touch someone without their consent again," the hooded man threatens in a deep, husky voice, "and you lose both hands, and then your life. Understand?"

The pervert nods frantically, tears falling freely down his face.

"Get out of my sight before I change my mind."

The man scurries out of the alley, not once looking back as he trips over himself trying to get away. After a few moments, my savior turns around. He's wearing a black mask over his features now, but I'd recognize him anywhere.

He pulls off the mask, and I gasp. Under the dark hood is Quentin, exactly as I remember him. He's older now, just like in my dreams and in the club. I'm speechless. Is this another moment of my brain playing tricks on me?

I breathe out his name, more as a question than anything. And suddenly, his lips are on mine. My entire body melts into his touch. It's the kiss I've been waiting for eleven years to happen. A kiss that's somehow everything I've ever wanted and all I've ever dreamt of. But just like all good things, it's over before I want it to be.

"You're mine," his deep voice whispers, and my eyes fly open. But he's gone, and I'm left standing alone in the empty alley.

CHAPTER 4
Quentin

I stalk quickly down the street, no aim or direction in mind. My mask dangles from my fingers, and I debate putting it back on. Somehow, I can't bring myself to do so. I've survived so long because of it, but yet somehow, putting it on seems wrong.

I hadn't meant to kiss her, but it just *happened*. And I'm not sorry that it did. Gemma is exactly how I expected her to be after all these years. Older, more mature, and yet still the same girl I used to have a raging crush on when I was sixteen.

I've been following her for a while. Maybe it's creepy; maybe I should be institutionalized, but it's the truth. It started off with morbid curiosity, and simply wanting to know how she's been doing. Then, I'd find her at places I didn't intend to look. I always stayed a healthy distance away; I have to stay away.

Until that jackass touched her. I wanted nothing more in that moment than to beat him into a pulp, but I didn't want Gemma to see that. So, I refrained, and I'm glad I did. Though I selfishly want her to myself, she deserves so much better than me.

I kick at a stone on the ground, watching as it skips across the sidewalk and falls into a gutter. By now, Gemma would be at home with her friend. Based on her state, I wonder if she'll be able to remember anything tomorrow. Perhaps it's for the best if she thinks all this is a dream and forgets me entirely.

I think back to the first time I saw her in this city. She was sitting in a coffee shop late at night, sipping a hot chocolate and talking with her friend. My heart stopped in my chest, and I remember almost falling to my knees at the sight of her through the window. I had to follow her then, to make sure she was living a good life far away from her horrible father. It elated me to find out that she lived in an apartment with the same friend she had been dining with.

That should have been the last time I saw her. But it wasn't. I found myself drawn to looking for her. I would wander the streets, looking for her even if I was supposed to do something else.

She's the one. I've always known she's the one for me. But I'm not the one for her; I'm not right. But this fact doesn't stop me from wanting her, from craving her.

Before I understand where I am or where I'm headed, I find myself before a fire escape. I've been here before, but I've never climbed up it. I know it's a bad idea to even think about going up, but I can't get my feet to move along. My brain screams for me to move along, to continue down the street as if nothing ever happened.

But my heart...

Suddenly, I'm nothing but wisps of shadow between the fabric of the world, and my form scales the wall with relative ease. Then, I'm perched before a windowsill, watching a figure stumble around her room in an attempt to change out of her skin-tight dress.

I have enough respect to turn away while she undresses, but glance back to see that she's wearing an oversized band T-shirt, her legs on full display. My fists clench, and I take three breaths.

I knock on the window without meaning to. Gemma freezes inches from the bed and turns, her eyes distant and dreamy.

"I can go if you'd like," I tell her. "Say the words, and I'm gone."

But she doesn't, and I know we're both screwed.

CHAPTER 5

Gemma

I'm having another dream again. I know because Quentin is here, tapping at my window with two knuckles. He tells me I have a choice, and that I can let him in or tell him to go. He says he'll be okay with either option, but he's not good for me. He's dangerous.

I tell him he's always been good for me. I've loved him since we were kids. I open the window, and he jumps inside with near-feline grace. When he stands at his full height, I know I should be intimidated, but I'm not. It's Quentin — *my* Quentin.

"I'm not good, Gemma," his husky voice tells me. I've been waiting so long to hear any words from him at all that I barely register their meaning.

"You're as good as I need you to be," I tell him, taking a singular step forward. "Please, don't leave again."

Something like guilt appears on his face, but it's gone in a blink. "Tell me to go."

"I can't do that," I tell him, swaying lightly on my feet.

He bares his teeth, and fangs replace where his canines should be. "I'm a vampire, Gemma. I'm as good as damned, cursed to walk the night, and the night alone."

I shake my head. "No. You're not damned."

He chuckles humorlessly. "I'm a *monster*, and you still want me?"

I nod, biting my bottom lip. I don't care what he is; I've only ever cared who he is. And Quentin is here, even if it is just a dream.

"I want you; I've always wanted you," I tell him, and it's the honest truth.

He curses, and some tether he had on himself snaps. With inhuman speed, he rushes toward me and slips his hands around my waist. He plants his lips on mine, and it feels just as enchanting as the first time. Sparks fly wherever his skin touches mine, and I swear that my heart is about to jump out of my chest.

My knees give out, but he catches me in his arms, holding me upright and allowing me to use him as a crutch. How can a dream feel as real as this? My answer comes moments later when he pulls away, only to dip his head to the side of my neck and sink his teeth into the soft flesh above my collarbone. It hurts, but only for a moment. My back arches, and I gasp, pleasure taking over my entire body. Heat travels to my core, and I need *more, more, more.*

"Quentin," I say with clarity. This isn't a dream — it never was.

He hums against my neck, the vibrations tickling my skin. I shudder.

"You're here," I say. A tear slips from my eye. "You're actually here."

He pulls away, and I see my blood on his teeth when he smiles. "I never left."

I choke back a sob. "You did. You left without saying goodbye, and you never came back. I waited for two years, *two years*, before moving here. No postcard, no letter, no email or message through a friend of a friend. Why?"

He's quiet for a few moments. "I just thought it would be better that way. Easier for you to move on."

"Well, I haven't!" I tell him, pounding a fist on his chest. He doesn't even flinch. "I never moved on, not truly."

He grimaces, and I take a step back. "You're a vampire."

With a nod, he steps back to put even more space between us. "Six years after I moved, I was turned."

"H-how?" I stutter. "How is this real?"

"It just is, Gemma. Either you accept it, or you don't."

I take a moment to let what he's saying sink in. I nod, the movement slight at first before turning more assertive. "Okay."

He's taken aback by this statement. "Okay? Just like that?"

"I trust you completely, Quentin. I know you'll never do anything to hurt me, so okay. Whoever — whatever — you are, I'll accept it."

He lets out a shaky breath. "I don't deserve you," he whispers.

"Good thing that's not up to you to decide." I exhale and close the gap between us again. I stand on my toes to kiss him and wrap my arms around his neck.

I open my mouth for him. I'm completely open to him, and that fact will never change.

Our clothes fall to the ground, and although we're moving fast, we've been waiting forever. Eleven years, I've waited for him, so when he lays me down on the bed, I'm not afraid.

"Are you sure about this?" he asks, nuzzling my neck.

"I've never been surer of something in my life," I assure him. He's the perfect match for me, inside and out. No other could ever begin to compare.

His thrusts light my entire being on fire. The pleasure is more than I've ever experienced, and I don't want it to end. But when the feeling intensifies, I find myself calling out his name while sparks explode in my vision.

We lie on my bed for a while. Though his breaths are even, I fight to catch my own.

"Stupid immortal stamina," I mutter, and he chuckles. He leans over me and pecks my lips before hauling himself from my bed and gathering his clothes that are scattered around the room.

"I can turn you immortal, like me," Quentin blurts out, slipping his shirt back over his head. "It's a simple process, though not entirely painless. I'd be by your side the entire time — if you want."

I sit up on my bed, clutching the sheets to my chest. "That's a heavy topic."

He shrugs and starts pulling on his black combat boots. "It's entirely your choice, but if you're... like me, I can protect you better. And we can be together, completely and forever."

"I know, but... *immortality*. That's a huge thing to ask me to make a decision on, Quentin. I can't... I can't just decide now."

He rushes over and tenderly grips my chin, forcing me to look up at him. "I'm not forcing you to make a decision now — or even tomorrow. You have an eternity to think about eternity and if you want it. I won't rush you, but I want to give you the option.

"Thank you," I tell him through a yawn. My eyes start to close on their own accord. "Please don't leave again."

His hand brushes the hair from my face. "I'll be here. Even if you can't see me, I'll still be here. I'll come back to you."

I don't have the chance to respond before sleep claims me.

CHAPTER 6
Quentin

Being a hunter myself, I know when I've turned into prey.

I weave in and out between buildings, blending into shadows and darkness, turning myself into the areas between the lamplights to move quickly along the alleyway. Still, the feeling of being followed chases me beyond comfort.

My chest heaves lightly when I stop to gather my

strength. Not all of my kind can do as I do and weave-step into the folds of darkness, but I've found it to be incredibly helpful when trying to avoid confrontations such as this.

I jump and wrap my fingers around a metal bar. I haul myself up and onto someone's balcony, balancing on the thin railing to reach the next. Within seconds, I'm on the roof, jumping across the gravel and trash that's accumulated up here. A flock of shorebirds squawk angrily as I race by. My mask presses into my face, and I don't know how anyone's recognized me with it on.

When I've rallied enough strength, I splay my arms wide and allow the darkness to consume my skin, seeping into my very being. I continue the same forward motion, shooting across a gap between the apartment buildings without falter. In this state, I have no body, no physical essence.

Then I'm whole again, standing on the edge of a rooftop and looking over the edge to where the street remains alive below. Cars dart back and forth across the road, and people bustle about, chatting or otherwise laughing amongst friends. The perfect cover.

I flick my hood up to cover my head, and I slip off the edge. My being vanishes from existence, only to reappear again when I land on the street. I walk casually, personifying a young man heading home after a long day. My steps become less perfect, and I hunch my shoulders to act as a human might.

But as I cross in front of an alley, a form appears beside me and shoves me backwards and into it. The next blow comes to the face, but I manage to dodge it, folding into darkness and stepping aside. But the man is instantly behind me. A blow comes to the back of my head, and I stumble forward. My mask is ripped off my face, and I feel exposed without it on.

Again and again, this man attacks me. Not to kill, but just to drain me enough that I can't use my power anymore. I know this because I was the one to teach him this method.

"Dante," I bark, straightening and facing the young vampire, who has his arm back and ready to strike. I stare into his blue-green eyes. Despite his shorter height, he's well-built and solid.

"Boss wants you," he says formally. There's no indication he's ever known me, no evidence in his voice that we might have once been friends. "Either you can come willingly, or I can finish what I've started. Your choice."

"Or," I snarl, baring my teeth at him, clenching my fists. "You can forget you've ever seen me. Pretend I got away, and nobody shall know."

He shakes his head. "Not happening."

"You know I can't go back there," I tell him, keeping my tone even. "I made my decision."

"And he made his." His raised fist doesn't so much as falter. "Don't make this harder than it has to be."

I stare at him for a heartbeat, and then allow myself to be taken into the darkness. But I don't move as he expects, and instead stay still until he teleports away. When he's out of reach, I bolt forward. But I'm exhausted, and my power is failing.

He hits me on the side of the face. My head snaps to one side, and my fangs slice through my bottom lip. Dark blood pours out, and I reach a hand up to wipe it away. I chuckle, not looking toward Dante.

"Someone taught you well, brother."

"You stopped meaning anything to me the moment you left."

Gemma's words flood back to me in that moment. Gemma, whom I also left eleven years ago but never stopped loving. Dante takes advantage of the distraction and grabs onto my arms. He ties them behind my back with cuffs designed by the leader of the vampires, Magnus himself. Crafted with some sort of substance to mimic sunlight, it's effective in rendering me absolutely powerless.

"You bastard," I say, spitting my blood at his feet. He ignores this, and simply pushes me further into the alley. "Let me go, Dante. He'll kill me."

"Maybe it's what you deserve." He says the words, but I can tell by his tone that he doesn't entirely mean it. What poisoned lies have they fed him?

He leads me over to a sewer grate and steps on it. It flips open, and he pushes it out of the way. It clatters against the ground, but he wastes no time in pushing me down and into the hole. I land on the ground, some twenty feet below. Even without the use of my hands, I'm able to catch my balance rather well.

Dante fixes the grate back into place and doesn't bother with the ladder. I see his eye through one of the holes, and he appears behind me, pushing me forward and into the darkness of the sewer tunnels.

It takes about five minutes to walk the length of the passages. I know them well, as I've myself traveled them thousands of times.

"When you see him, don't do anything stupid," Dante hisses in my ear when we come to a large iron door. It looks ancient and rusted with a skull inscribed in the center. To a human, it would appear sealed off or even hazardous. But to us, it means home. "Sanguis," Dante says. I raise an eyebrow, and he adds to me, "He had the password changed after you left. Precautions. You understand."

The door swings open, the hinges creaking and echoing along the tunnels. On the other side, the hallway looks like a manor. A red carpet runs along the length of the tunnel, and the wooden walls are decorated in frames and lanterns.

"Thanks, Barth," Dante says to the man on the other side of the door. Barth, a tall and lanky vampire with no special ability beyond being one to piss people off, nods in affirmation.

We walk down the hallway with no sound beyond our feet hitting the ground. We round the corner, and I can hear talking come from behind the door at the end of the hall. As we get closer, I can make out Magnus' voice barking orders at someone. Nothing has changed.

Dante raises a fist to the door and knocks three times. The chatting from inside ceases, and Magnus' voice calls, "Enter."

The door swings open, and we step inside. The large throne room is exactly as I remember it to be. Two long tables line the red carpet that continues up to the silver chair where Magnus is perched. Guards stand around the room, but there is no indication of who Magnus was just talking to.

"Ah, Quentin. Glad to have you back," he says, standing and stretching out his arms with a wide grin. I glare, my own hands still secured tightly behind me. "I'm sorry about my methods of bringing you here; but you see, you're a tricky man to find."

"In case it wasn't clear enough when I left, I'll say it now," I say, lowering my brows. "I'm sick of being your pawn. I've left the guild, and you won't have to see me again."

His smile drops, and he matches my frown. "You've cost me a lot. You need to stay and repay that debt."

"I don't owe you *shit*!" I bellow. "Find another heir. It'll be easy for you, considering that you've turned about half the vampires in this place."

"And what great additions to the family they are," he croons, then smiles at Dante behind me. "Thank you for bringing him to me. Your mother is free to go."

There it is. I knew Dante wouldn't be capable of going after me in such a manner without an outside influence.

Dante bows and goes to leave, but Magnus calls after him, "Tell Arabella I wish to see her."

I wonder what Arabella has to do with anything, but that isn't the first question I want answered. When my former friend has left the throne room, I strain against my binds to test how fragile they might be. They hold true, and I internally curse Dante for not giving me a way out.

"You know, when I heard of your rebellion, I was shocked," Magnus says, walking down the steps and toward me. If he comes close enough, I promise myself I'll bury my teeth in his neck and damn the consequences. "I mean—it couldn't be true! My own heir, whom I've come to think of as a son to me, abandoned his people."

"They're your people, not mine," I remind him. "I never wanted the throne."

"Ah, but that's where you're wrong." Magnus stops just out of reach, taunting me, daring me to try and go for him. "You love power. You *crave* it. It's more freedom you want, isn't it? Leading is the ultimate freedom. I was simply helping you get there."

No. I'm about to lash out, scream at him or worse, but the door Dante disappeared behind opens once more. A tall woman walks out, although still shorter than me. Her long red hair bounces with her walk, and her skin is as white as snow. Arabella.

Magnus pulls her into his side and kisses her on the cheek. "Before you left, my daughter here brought up a very good point. What better way to solidify you as my heir than to have a union of marriage?" He laughs, as if the whole concept was as simple as getting a new suit. "I'll admit, I wasn't exactly a fan of the idea at first. But she convinced me that this sort of bond would be perfect for the order. My son, not just by kinship, but by marriage as well." He claps his hands together as if the whole arrangement has just been finalized.

"No," I state simply. "I won't marry her for any reason, but least of all because you think it'll keep me complacent."

I spare a look to Arabella. Throughout the entire exchange, her face has remained completely neutral, as if her mind is someplace else. The only indication she's actually listening is a tiny facial twitch after my statement.

"I'm not staying," I remind him. "There is nothing you can do or say that will make me change my mind."

His eyes narrow into slits. "I've been patient with you,

Quentin. I've even let your parents live peaceful lives outside the city."

I feel the blow as if he had physically punched me. My parents *are* still alive on the orders of Magnus. I've tried to move them a few times, but since they think I'm dead... indirectly telling them to leave their house is turning out to be trickier than I imagined. Despite this, I've taken many measures to make sure no vampire will come within a hundred yards of their home.

"I'd hate if something were to happen to them," Magnus says, running his hand along his daughter's arm. "But that's just me."

"Blackmail me all you want," I say. "My parents mean little to me now. They'll be dead in a few decades anyway. What does it matter?" Of course, I'm lying about all this. I care greatly that I will likely outlive my parents hundreds of times over.

"I don't need blackmail," Magnus says, grinning to show off his canines. Though his tone is casual, I know better than to assume that he's harmless. "You'll come around eventually."

I just laugh and shake my head. He can try anything he wants; I've already gone through it all. Magnus is extremely thorough with all his blackmailing, and the only reason I got out the last time was because I made some very large sacrifices. "Good luck."

The Lord of the Vampires snaps his fingers, and two men rush forward, each grabbing one of my elbows. I fight against them, but only for a moment. I know any attempt to free myself with these cuffs on would be idiotic. I'll just wait until I'm alone in whatever cell he throws me into, and

I'll try to cut them off. I'll do so with my teeth if I have to. Nothing is flawless, and I'll find a weakness. I have to.

I'm escorted out of the room and through a tunnel that leads down into the chambers below. This space isn't nearly as well decorated as above, partly because Magnus doesn't care about the people he throws down here, and otherwise, because it's the oldest part of the underground building. In fact, the original purpose *was* to hold vampires captive.

Fortunately for me, I'm not an average vampire.

"Here you are," one of the men, whom I don't recognize at all, says. "Boss had it made specially for you."

I'm left confused only for a moment, when a solid iron door opens and reveals an all-white room. Lights shine from spaces in every direction, and the first thing I notice is that there are no shadows, no areas of darkness at all.

The man throws me inside and closes the door behind himself without another word.

I'm stunned. The lights aren't ultraviolet so my skin doesn't burn, but I'm rendered completely powerless even if I do manage to get the cuffs off.

I scream. My last defense has just been cut off, and I know I won't be able to leave this room without Magnus' word. But I won't fold; I can't go back to that old life of murder and exploitation.

I need a plan.

THE DOOR CREAKS OPEN, AND I FLINCH AT THE sound. I'm propped upright in the corner against the padded wall, my hands still bound tightly behind myself.

Magnus walks inside, and the door shuts behind him. He crouches down to me and uses a long, spindly finger to brush a strand of black hair from my eyes. "You're evasive; I'll give you that."

My face turns into a sneer, and I pull away from his touch. "You can't force me to be your heir. One day, you'll make a mistake, and I'll either kill you or leave."

"You see, I don't think so," the cocky monster says, standing up and straightening. "You see, a little birdy told me that you have a mate. Gemma, her name is? Well, I've got to say, she's very lovely. I'd hate for something to happen to her."

I stop. My entire world stops. He knows about Gemma? Does he have her? She wouldn't be dead already; he'll hang this over my head until she isn't useful to him anymore. "You touch her, and I'll burn this entire city to the ground." It's not a threat; it's a promise.

Magnus must see the sincerity in my eyes because he says, "I don't doubt that." He smirks and places a hand on his chest. "Which is why I've put round-the-clock protection on her. That way, she'll be safe."

I curse at him, threatening him with every bit of aggression I feel. I want to lash out at him, rip his head from his shoulder. I want to watch as he dies, but I know that the moment he perishes, Gemma's life is on the line. He has likely made many precautions to ensure he walks out of this room alive.

"You should think about what I've said," Magnus says, straightening the lapels on his jacket and turning to leave.

"You'll never hold me, Magnus," I tell him. "One day,

I'll get free with Gemma by my side, and you'll regret every decision you've ever made."

He turns around when he reaches the threshold. "I look forward to it."

The door slams shut, sealing me off from the world once again.

CHAPTER 7
Gemma

The events of last night were... unreal.

I stare at myself in the mirror, eyes fixated on the near-concealed twin puncture marks on the one side of my neck. With my pounding headache and twisted stomach, I almost thought when I woke up that the entire thing was a vivid figment of my imagination. But no; of course, the twin wounds are a constant reminder of my infidelity toward Jayden.

The worst part about it is that I don't feel guilty about

the entire thing. Perhaps it makes me a terrible person; perhaps it proves that Jayden is way too good for me. I don't care either way.

"Pretty nice tips today," Shelly says from her vanity a few spots to my right. She wears nothing but a bra while she counts the stack of cash. "Also, I heard that you had a pretty wild night yesterday."

I cringe at the thought, and unscrew my concealer to reapply to the side of my neck. My tips are in my bag, already counted and banded. "Don't remind me."

"Hey, we've all been there," she says, raising her hands into the air. "Your boyfriend got a vampire kink or something?"

"What?" I ask, smearing the concealer over the spots and bringing out my blending brush. "No!"

"Whatever, I don't judge," she says, shooting me a wink.

I chuckle, and finish blending the mark on my neck. My phone vibrates, and it's Jayden, telling me that he won't be able to pick me up tonight as his meeting is running late. He goes on to explain that he'll be able to come get me later for dinner, though. I don't mind, as I had to take the bus this morning as well.

I gather up my things and say goodbye to Shelly, who waves at me and tells me to always use protection. Apart from Micaela, she's my closest friend. She knows the deepest things about me, even though we've never met up outside of work hours.

When I step out of the club, I see a familiar car on the side of the road. My heart hammers in my chest, and I dip my head, turning and walking quickly in the opposite direction.

"Gemma!" Micaela's voice is followed by the slamming of that car's door. *Shit.* "Gemma, wait!"

I stop in my tracks. I'm not exactly sure how I'm going to explain my way out of this one. "Hey, Micaela! What are you doing here?" I ask, spinning around to face her. She beckons me over, and I hesitate before walking over to her car.

"Do you work here?" She gestures to Temptation. "Be honest with me."

I can't read the emotions on her face, but it doesn't look good. I toe at the ground, unable to meet her eye. "Yes."

"Why didn't you tell me?" she asks, raising her palms to the sky. People around turn and stare. "Don't you trust me?"

"Get in the car," I tell her, pushing her toward the driver's side. "Just—get in, and we'll talk."

She huffs but complies, sliding into the driver's seat and slamming the door behind herself. I walk around to the other side and take my time opening the passenger's door. How am I supposed to explain?

Once I get in, Micaela immediately jumps on me again. "I mean, I had to follow you all the way from the bus stop this morning to find out. How long have you been lying to me?"

"There's no job at the restaurant," I mutter softly. "Never was."

She takes a deep breath. "So, for years, then."

"It's not like that!" Blood rushes to my face. "I'm sorry, Micaela. I never meant to hurt you."

"No? Well, you've done a poor job of showing that."

"Why did you follow me?" I ask, confused on why she would do such a thing. Something would have had to tip her off.

She turns and glares in my direction. "Don't make this about me—"

"No," I say, waving my hand. "I'm not mad you did, just... curious."

She leans back in her seat, closing her eyes, though her jaw is still clenched. It looks like she's trying to keep herself from crying. I run my hand along the dash, clearing some of the dust away. "I had a feeling. All your fancy clothes and heels, your perfect makeup routine, and the fact that you sometimes come home covered in glitter. Then when we went out last night... you knew way too much about how the place operates. I didn't want to confront you about it in case I was wrong, but—*God*, Gemma, why didn't you just tell me?"

"I'm ashamed of it," I state honestly. "I couldn't get another job in time for rent, so originally, it was supposed to be a temporary thing. But then I saw how good the tips were, and a few months turned into a year, which turned into... this."

"You should have told me."

"I didn't know how you would react. And telling you... it made it all too real, somehow. I didn't want you to see me as whore."

"Never," Micaela says, and I feel her hand on my shoulder. I look up, and there are definitely tears in her eyes. "I'd never see you that way. I just... please tell me things from now on?"

I nod, and I mean it. "Of course."

"I could have helped you. With the rent, you know."

"I know. I couldn't ask that of you." I take her hand off my shoulder and hold it in my own. "I'm truly sorry. Can you forgive me?"

She smiles. "Always."

~

"You're sure what I'm wearing is okay?" I ask Jayden for the hundredth time. "It's just—I haven't seen your family in a while. Does this dress say 'sorry for ghosting everyone'?"

He chuckles and shakes his head. "You're beautiful. Besides, it's too late to change now." He kisses my forehead and takes my hand in his. We continue up the steps into a small little mom and pop diner. He holds open the door for me, and I step inside.

I'm immediately hit with the smell of fries and different pastas. I've never been here before, but it looks cozy. Wooden tables of various size and shapes line the room, and the hanging yellow lights provide a dim atmosphere.

"There they are," Jayden declares, and points to where a couple and their daughter are already sitting, waiting. Jayden's mother is lovely, with the same brown hair as her son. Theresa is tall and petite, with a wide smile that lights up any room. Jayden is the splitting image of his father, except the hair. His father, Doug, is ginger like his daughter, and has kind hazel eyes.

"Hi, everyone, thanks for having me," I tell them, and

we exchange pleasantries while I slide into the chair beside Jayden. "Lucia, I hear you were accepted into college?"

Jayden's sister nods enthusiastically. "I'm thinking of taking history, but I'm still on the fence about it."

"That's amazing," I tell her. "Congratulations."

When the server comes and asks for our drinks, I request a sweet tea. It's the best drink choice, and nobody can tell me otherwise.

"I'll take a Bloody Mary," Theresa requests last, and I stiffen.

"You okay?" Jayden mutters to me, and I nod.

Blood.

I'm reminded of Quentin, and everything that happened last night. How can I sit here and pretend to be a part of this family, pretend to love Jayden, when I cheated on him with an immortal man I've been pining after for years of my life? My hand instinctively goes up to my neck, but I force it back to the table.

"Are you alright, dear? You look pale." Theresa shoots a concerned frown in my direction.

"Yeah," I say, feigning a smile. "I'll—uh... I'll be back."

I take off, and don't allow myself to breathe until I've entered the restroom. The door swings shut behind me, and I step over to the sink. I turn it on, allowing the cold water to run for a few moments before splashing it over my face. Then, I swear when I remember the marks on my neck.

They're still mostly covered, but I can definitely tell there's something there. After a moment of thinking, I take the clip from my hair and allow the strands to fall down around my neck. I pull my hair to that side, and cringe at the attempt. It's better than nothing, but I'll have to be careful.

Maybe I should just tell Jayden what happened. He deserves to know, after all. *I* would want to know if the roles were reversed.

I can't. It would devastate him. And if I swear to myself that I'll never see Quentin again, I can forget about this entire situation and go back to pretending my childhood crush never existed.

But I don't want *that*, either.

I take another few deep breaths, and pat my face dry with some pieces of paper towel.

Just then, the bathroom door opens. "It's just me," Lucia's voice says, and she slips inside. "Is everything okay?"

"Yeah," I answer. "I've just had a rough couple of days."

"Hangover?" When my eyes go wide, she chuckles. "Just a good guess."

"Don't tell anyone, okay? Don't want to ruin my reputation." I'm glad for the out; I'm not sure what I would have said to explain my situation.

She rolls her eyes. "What reputation?"

I playfully nudge her shoulder. I say sarcastically, "*Thanks*, kid."

"We should go back out there. I think they're getting ready to order soon."

And when I head back out, I decide on two things. One, I'm not going to tell Jayden about last night. And two, the hardest part, is that I have to give up Quentin.

CHAPTER 8

Quentin

"Good news, Quentin. I've got a mission for you," Magnus tells me when I arrive in the throne room, my hands still bound behind my back. One of his guards nudges me forward, and I want nothing more than to get my hands on him and snap him neck.

"I don't know how efficient I'll be without the use of my hands or powers," I retort dryly.

"The cuffs are just a precaution until you're out of the building. Now, Dante will escort you—"

"*Escort*?" I demand with a laugh. "No. I work alone. Always have, always will."

"Don't interrupt me!" he shouts, standing from his chair. I flinch back, and Magnus' brows lower over his eyes. "Dante will be joining you, and that is not up for debate. Additionally, I will have guards posted along your route, so if one or both of you fail to meet the checkpoints... well, you can imagine what will happen to your precious mate."

I keep my eyes shut and settle on simply glaring at the man. Years' worth of hatred is poured into my gaze, but if he's fazed, he doesn't show any of it.

"Dante has the details of the mission. If you please." Magnus waves his arm, and Dante steps out from his spot along the wall. I hadn't even noticed his presence in the room.

My former friend grabs my upper arm and pulls me toward the large doorway that leads out and into the hallway. I don't fight him; in all honesty, I'm glad to be leaving this place. I know the only reason I'm going is so that Magnus feels some semblance of control over me again. Get me doing grunt work, get me compliant, and I'll be less likely to attack him at the first chance I get. Well, he's dead wrong.

"Look, man. *Please* don't try anything. Let's just have this go smoothly, and nobody gets hurt."

I don't respond. He can go to hell, for all I care.

We make it into the sewer and, before long, we're out on the street. Only then does Dante unbind my hands, and

I rub my wrists as my power slowly floods back into my possession.

"So, what are we doing?" I ask, surveying the alley we popped out of. It's not the same one we went down the night before. A rat scuttles under the dumpster, and there's graffiti on the brick walls. My eyes dart all around until I'm sure I've drank in every small detail.

"Pick up," Dante deadpans. I know exactly what he means, and I refrain from groaning. It's the worst sort of job in every way possible. I've never actually done it myself, but I've heard from some of the newer members that it's pretty terrible. "Let's go."

I sigh, but follow him into the street. We blend in decently well with the crowd, despite my all-black outfit and cloak. Luckily, Magnus allowed me to have my mask back, though had it tucked into one of the pockets within my cloak. I fish it out before sliding it over my features, concealing my identity from anyone who were to look in my direction. All of my concealed blades are still on me, which isn't surprising. Magnus likes to play mind games, and I'm sure this is one of them.

"I'm sorry about this," Dante says, leaning in to mutter the words as we step around a couple of teenagers. I don't say anything, and he goes on. "You know I didn't have a choice, right?"

"Of course, you had a choice," I mutter. "You always have a choice."

"Not really. You know he had my mother, but he has my parents every single day. One word, and they're dead."

I stop and glare at him, and I know my eyes are just visible through the slits in the mask. "I have parents, too, you know. *And* a mate. But I still find a way to defy him because *I can't live like that anymore.*"

"I understand—"

"No, you don't!" I snap. "You've always been happy being his lapdog. He calls, and you come."

"Not since you left." He says this with such finality that I'm rendered speechless. He continues walking down the street, and I have no choice but to follow. "When you made the decision to leave, Magnus punished the rest of us for it. He thought there was going to be some sort of rebellion, and he became more paranoid than ever. Since then, I've been doing these sorts of jobs, hunting down, and sometimes killing, those he thinks are a threat. I've... I've had to kill some parents, too. All to keep proving my loyalty."

I don't know what to say. We turn a few corners, and the streets become less and less crowded. Until it's just us on a dead street in the middle of a sleeping town.

"I'm sorry you had to do that," I say finally. "You shouldn't have had to."

"No," he agrees. "And if you had stayed, everything would be fine. If you kept your promise to take over the clan when he steps down, you could have made things different for all of us."

"He never would have allowed that," I say quietly. "He never wanted to step down; he just wanted me as insurance that if he were to die, he'd have a successor. And if I stayed with him until that point... I would have lost myself, Dante. You have to understand that."

It's his turn to stay silent. We make a few more turns around the streets until we come to an old, rundown building covered in vines. I raise a brow. "It looks like it's about to collapse at any moment. No way there are humans in there."

Dante sends me a contemptuous look and disappears from view. I look around frantically, and see he's entered the building through a slit in the boards covering the window. "Better than knocking on the front door."

I roll my eyes and fold into the shadows. When I reappear, I'm standing next to him. My boot crunches on a broken piece of glass, and I instantly don't want to be here anymore. "Can you tell me *anything*?" I hiss in his ear.

Dante shakes his head, a sly smile appearing on his face. "It's more fun this way. Now, take off your mask. Leave the cloak on, though. I think it sells the whole thing better."

I huff, but pull off my beloved mask. Although it's a bit unnecessary now that they've all found me, I find it adds a sense of security and anonymity that's comforting.

No sooner than I took off my mask did Dante's fist come flying and hit me square on the cheekbone.

"What the fuck?" I ask, taking a few steps back and reaching a hand up to touch my face. I'm almost certain that it'll give me a black eye. "If you wanted to have a go, you could have gone for the stomach or something."

Dante pouts, mockingly. "Oh, are you worried that your little mate won't find you attractive anymore? Calm down, I needed to roughen you up a little — your broken lip is almost healed. Just trust me."

"Rich, coming from the man who just punched me in the face," I grumble, but I follow Dante down the corridor.

I come to realize that it used to be a small office building of sorts, based on the plethora of adjoining rooms off the hallway. I peer through one window to see that the room is absolutely trashed, though there is a single grimy mattress atop all the broken glass and smashed electronics. There's no sight of the owner, and I'm not sure if I want to meet them.

What sort of humans are we picking up?

Eventually, we make it to a heavy metal door. Through the surprisingly intact frosted glass window, I see the dark outline of a large man. Dante lifts his fist and knocks on the door. Moments later, it swings open to reveal a large, round man wearing black jeans and a short black shirt. Certainly not someone I'd expect in a place like this.

"You pay at the front already?" the man asks, looking between us. "Who's the fighter?"

My gaze snaps to Dante, who clears his throat. "We did, and that's him. I'm his coach."

The man looks me up and down before settling to look at my face. I know what I must look like, a pale, battered up kid in his mid-twenties. I match the man's gaze and straighten my spine. I'm lean and about a head taller than Dante, but that's not usually the first thing people notice about me.

When, at last, the bouncer steps aside to let us in, I shoot another look at Dante. He pointedly ignores me. The two of us descend a set of steep, wooden stairs. The further we go down, the louder I hear the roaring and cheering of people.

"*Fighter?*" I ask, grabbing his shoulder. "You didn't say anything about fighting."

"Oh, relax. You'll be a natural, I promise. Just... don't do any of that shadow stuff. You know the rules."

"*No humans are to know that we're vampires or have the*

slightest indication of our abilities." I mock Magnus' droning tone. "Whatever."

When we enter the main room, it's insane. There are three different pits with two fighters each, beating each other to a pulp with their bare fists. Standing all around and up on the balconies are people watching and yelling, waving money in the air.

Underground fighting rings. I've purposefully avoided these for a reason.

The walls are all made of stone, and the ground is gray concrete, with red pads in the areas where the fighting rings are. Faded paint lines are in some places around the room, but they're long past the point of recognition.

Dante pulls me into a corner as we observe the chaos around us. "Goal is to get a fighter and his coach to come with us after the match. For that reason, you'll have to make it a *good* fight, and not get on the fighter's bad side. You'll offer to teach him a few things."

"Why not just swipe a few people off the street and be done with it?" I groan. "Avoid all this."

"It's always been done this way. Take people from the underground; that way, nobody's going to want to snitch that they're gone. Shady things happen here all the time; it won't be as suspicious."

I roll my eyes, but it does make sense. As much as a kidnapping plot could make sense.

"Do you see anyone you want to go against?" he asks, and I take the time to look around again. The fighters and their coaches are pretty distinctive; fighters often have their shirts off and are peppered in cuts and bruises.

"I'd prefer to leave," I say honestly.

"Not an option. How about... that guy with the beard over there?"

I glance at who he's talking about. He's an older, gruff man with a long, brown beard. Even so, he's muscled and large. "No."

Dante sighs. "Well, then you choose."

I look around again. I know I could take all the people here at once if I really wanted to, but that's not what I'm screening for. I'm looking for someone who I know I won't be quite as guilty for sending to a death sentence.

It's all for Gemma, I remind myself. Sacrificing two lives for hers will be nothing. I'm willing to burn down the whole world for her if I need to.

"Them," I say, pointing at a thirty-year-old man with shoulder-length blonde hair. He's shaking hands with a former opponent, but I can tell from here that he's gripping his opponent's hand a little too hard based on the sneer on his face. Next to him is his coach, a skinny balding man taking a stack of cash from another coach.

Dante cracks his knuckles. "Let's go, then. Keep your mouth shut, and let me do the talking."

We pick our way across the floor, avoiding people pushing into each other to get better views of the fights. When we get over there, the blonde fighter sneers at me. I'm about the same height as him, but he's twice as wide. I don't back down from his glare and simply look him up and down, feigning boredom.

"What's it going to take?" Dante asks the balding man. "I've got an opponent."

"Names?" the coach asks, chewing gum and not looking up from counting his money.

"I'm Daz, and this is... Stultus." My mind reels at the fake name he's given me. I know Latin pretty well, and he's going to pay for the insult.

At last, the coach looks up, smacking his gum. "I'm Hurley. This is Harley. What's your offer?" They're obviously not real names, but neither are ours. Someone would be foolish to hand out their true names in a place like this.

Dante — or *Daz* — reaches into his pocket and pulls out a wad of cash. "Three hundred."

The man's eyes flash, and he waves at someone across the room. A stout man bounces over, keys jangling from his belt loop. "What's up, Hurley?"

"Got another," he says, smacking his gum as he speaks. "Three-hundo."

The stout man looks to Dante. "Big spender, huh? What are your names?"

My *coach* first points to himself, and then to me. "Daz and Stultus."

"First time?"

Dante nods. "First time here, yeah. We're from out of town. Used to fight at a club downtown."

The stout man's eyes narrow. "Anywhere I know?"

Dante doesn't miss a beat. "Calcar's?"

"Oh, how is the old fella? Haven't seen him in years!"

As Dante goes on, I find myself surprised at the amount of background information he has on underground fighting rings. Perhaps I don't know him as well as I thought.

After the coaches both hand over the respective cash, I pull Dante aside. "*Stultus*? You just *had* to call me stupid in Latin."

He shrugs, a smile appearing on his face. "Make fun where you can."

I shed my cloak and hand it over to Dante. Then, reluctantly, take off the crisscross leather straps across my chest, then my shirt. I've always been well-built, but since becoming a vampire, I've only gotten even more defined.

Harley whistles at me from across the ring. "Lookin' good, kiddo!"

I turn to Dante. "You owe me for this."

He shakes his head, smiling wide. "Just don't let me lose that money."

I refrain from rolling my eyes. No chance in that.

It doesn't take long for the two of us to climb into the ring and for the fight to start. Rules are simple: no weapons, no death blows, and the first person to render their partner incapacitated wins.

Harley lunges first. I step easily out of the way, bouncing on the balls of my feet. I roll my neck and grin at the man, who glares in my direction. Maybe this will be fun.

I land the first blow, straight to his jaw. I pull my punch by a lot, else he might have been completely annihilated. His head snaps back, and blood sprays from his mouth.

He curses at me and rushes forward. I dodge again, and my elbow finds its way buried in his back. I look up, and my eyes meet Dante, who frowns and shakes his head at me. I take a deep breath. He's right; I can't get too carried away.

I let him get a few hits in. One to my stomach, and two more to my face. None of them land very well, although I know they'll likely bruise. Back and forth, we send punches.

At one point, I allow him to get me into a headlock before throwing him over my shoulder.

I'm doing this for Gemma. I'm doing this for Gemma.

"You fight like a woman," Harley taunts, spitting blood at my feet.

"I happen to know some very competent women," I tell him, and he doesn't stand a chance.

"I TOLD YOU TO GET HIM TO RESPECT YOU!" Dante says as we stand outside the building on the street. "Not beat him up so badly that nobody else will fight you. God, Magnus is going to be *so* pissed—"

I hiss at him to shut up and, surprisingly, he does. I strain my ears to pick up any slight movement on the street, listening intently. I've thankfully put my clothes back on, though I can't don the mask since it rubs abrasively against my nose, which was dislocated until Dante popped it back into place for me.

It doesn't take long for me to hear the familiar scuffle of shoes on pavement. I gesture toward the other side of the building. "There you go, all for you."

"Hey kid, why don't I give you a taste of a true fight?"

It's Harley and Hurley, back for more. Dante disappears from his place and reappears behind the two men. He leans down and bites the crook of Harley's neck, only lightly sinking his teeth into flesh.

"What the—" Hurley starts, but Dante is on him. After the bite to the neck, both men are rendered in a blissful, euphoric state. He ties their hands behind their backs and urges them forward. Hurley trips over his own feet, his face turned up in a lazy smile. "Did you just... bite us?"

"Whatever you laced that stuff with is killer," Harley says, swaying lightly. "Where are we going?"

"You have no idea," I grumble and urge them forward. Dante tells me it's about two blocks before the closest sewer, so we have to try and inconspicuously move them until then.

"I have to give it to you; you're pretty clever," Dante tells me, throwing an arm around Hurley and attempting to look like a friend helping his drunk acquaintance back home.

"Thanks?" I lilt, attempting to hold Harley upright.

We scuffle down the streets as fast as we can move. Luckily, there aren't that many people out anymore; pretty much everyone is asleep.

But then, a voice catches my attention.

"—next week for sure. Alright, you take care. Drive safe, Doug."

It's Gemma. My eyes dart across the street to see her standing on the side of the road with another man, waving at an older couple and their daughter as they drive off. Once the car is out of sight, the man bends over and plants a kiss on her mouth.

My heart shatters into a million pieces. How could I have expected a lovely woman such as her to not be taken? So incredibly foolish I was to think that I, a murderous monster, could possibly win her heart.

"Is that her?" Dante asks softly, following my gaze.

Gemma laughs at something the man says. The sound is one I want to hear forever until the end of time. "Yes."

"Oh man, I'm sorry," he says, then grunts under the weight of his human, who has fallen asleep.

Gemma gets into a car with that man, and they drive away.

I'm going to kill him; I'm going to kill him—

"I have to go after her," I say, allowing the human to fall in a heap to the ground. I start in the direction of the car. "What if she's in trouble?"

Dante appears in front of me, a hand upon my chest. "She looked pretty willing to me."

"Get out of my way," I utter, folding into the darkness around me and going around him.

"I can't do that," he tells me, and blocks me again. "Please don't make me put the cuffs on you."

Again, the shadows consume me, and I shoot backwards and around.

"If you don't make it back, Magnus will kill her and your family," Dante calls.

I pause. He's right, and I know he's right, but... "Give me a few hours. Please?"

He sighs, checking his watch. "They have security on her, but I'll think of something. Magnus isn't expecting us for a while, but hurry. If you're not back here in two and a half hours, I'm going straight to the clan and telling them everything."

"Thanks, Dante. You won't regret it, I promise. I'll be back as soon as I can."

"I bloody hope so," is his response.

CHAPTER 9

Gemma

There's a knock on my window, and I know there's only one person it could be. I finish taking off my shoes and jacket, and throw them onto the bed. Sure enough, when I turn toward the fire escape, Quentin is there. His hunched figure is clad in the same cloak as last night.

I sigh, before walking over and unlatching the window, heaving it open with both hands.

"Can I come in?" he asks, and I step aside. He crawls

through, landing silently on my floor. He shoves his hands into his pockets and looks around, even though he's been here before. Finally, his body turns to face me, and his eyes land on mine. I'm shocked to see his face is peppered in bruises and cuts. Instinctively, I walk over and reach a hand up to cup his jaw.

"What happened?"

He leans into my touch. "Just a friend of mine's cruel idea of a joke."

"I don't like this friend, then."

His mouth quirks up into a grin. "It's alright. I deserved it. Listen, I have to talk to you about something."

I pull my hand away. I close it into a fist, unsure what to do with it after. "What is it?"

"I saw you with a man. Leaving a restaurant. He... kissed you."

My face heats. "Jayden."

"The bastard has a name?"

"He's my boyfriend!" I tell him quickly. "He's my boyfriend, and he loves me."

"Do you love him?"

I bite my lip. Sure, I've *told* Jayden I love him, but is it real? Is it anything close to the love I feel for the one before me?

He grumbles, "Thought so," before taking a step back. "I need you to choose, Gemma."

"Choose what? Between you two?!" It's a completely rational request, and yet my temper boils at the thought of it. Quentin is my everything; he's what I've always wanted... but Jayden is peace; he's safety and security. He's the family I've never truly had.

"Yes, Gemma. Choose between the two of us." He flashes his fangs, but I'm not scared. I could never be scared of him.

"I can't choose! You came back into my life *yesterday* and dropped this huge idea that you're a *vampire* and all that! I don't know what to say or do about that information! I have a job, Quentin. I have a life here, and I'm... happy." I don't know why my mouth tripped over that last word, but I bite the inside of my cheek. "I'm happy," I say softly. I'm not sure who I'm trying to convince more — him or me.

He gestures to himself. "*This* is what I am, Gemma!" He takes off his hood and bares his teeth again. He runs his tongue along his elongated canines. "You want to know what to think about it?"

Quentin disappears, but I can still hear his heavy breathing in the room. When he reappears, he's standing behind me, his breath fanning my ear.

"I'm not afraid of you," I tell him breathlessly. "I just... give me time. Please?"

"Unfortunately, we don't exactly have the luxury of time," he says softly. My brows draw together, and I turn around.

"What do you mean?"

"I work for a very bad... *man*. Of my kind. He wants you dead for what you are to me, who you are. He says that if I don't do as he says, he'll kill you." He takes a deep, shuddering breath. "I'm so sorry, Gemma."

I press a hand to his chest. "Are you in danger?" He laughs, and I tilt my head. "What's so funny?"

"I just told you that someone wants you dead, and

you're worried about *my* safety?" He takes a step back. "Just —be safe, okay?"

"Don't go," I plead. As much as I'm conflicted about my feelings, I don't want him to leave me.

"Sweetheart, you're the bane of my existence," he says, and just like that, he's gone.

I spin around multiple times, trying to see if he will reappear somewhere else in my bedroom. But I know he's gone. I can no longer feel his presence like the lifeblood within me. He's electric; he's everything.

I fall down onto the bed. I don't know what to do. I wish everything wasn't so complicated.

Another knock, but this time, it's coming from my door. Micaela enters with a yawn. A robe hangs loosely over her shoulders. "What the hell's going on in here?"

CHAPTER 10

Quentin

"You guys are really nice," Harley says breathlessly as we wander the various tunnels.

"Shut up," Dante and I say simultaneously. We share a look, and Hurley snores from his place over my friend's shoulder.

I step over a dead rat, but the human trips over its carcass. "What was *that*?"

"Dead rat," I tell him. I turn to the vampire by my side. "I forgot how annoying humans are after you bite them."

"You're just jealous of my venom," he says, grinning. "Besides, didn't you feed during the time you were gone?"

"Not on humans," I admit. I *did* bite Gemma, and although she did feel euphoric, it was nothing to the extent of this. But that's just because she's my mate, and venom hardly works on a vampire's human mate. It's something about the connection forged between us. I didn't really pay attention when Magnus gave me the rundown of my abilities so long ago.

When we finally arrive at the front doors, I'm surprised that Dante doesn't put the cuffs back on. I don't say anything, and we continue inside down the long corridor in silence.

Back in the throne room, I feel my throat close up. I've always hated this room and the man that presides over it. Magnus sits on his glorified chair, smiling down at us and the humans in our grasp.

"I was beginning to think the two of you would never return," he says with a wide smile. "Leave them there."

Dante places Hurley on the ground, and I nudge Harley to his knees. The two mortals look helpless, although they don't even know they're in a room where they're a meal.

Magnus snaps his fingers, and everyone in the room except him, Dante, and I rush forward to devour the two humans. I look away, unable to watch the carnage.

I almost don't see Magnus come up beside me and place a hand on my shoulder. "Come with me."

My eyes narrow. "Why?"

He cocks his head. "You don't exactly have a choice, do you? I'd like to have dinner with you, for old time's sake."

I allow him to lead me from the room. I shoot Dante a pleading look, but he averts his eyes to the ground.

The dining hall is gigantic. Its purpose is to hold all the vampires within the clan at once. There are two long tables with an aisle in the middle, then one perpendicular at the top. The entire place is empty, though I'm not surprised. Vampires don't have to eat every day, and feeding together is only ever done for special occasions.

A red carpet lines the middle, though it wasn't always this color. Above, attached to the high ceiling, is a massive crystal chandelier that looks way too heavy to be supported by the wooden ceiling, but yet, here it's stood for, as I understand it, over three centuries.

"Favier, two pints, if you please," he says to one of the lower vampires who acts as a servant and cook for the compound. Anyone that Magnus himself doesn't sire, or doesn't have a power, is considered lower and insignificant. He only ever bothers with the "special" cases.

"What do you want to talk about?" I ask when we both sit down at the furthermost table, opposite from each other.

"Straight to it, huh? That's my boy, always getting to the point." He folds his hands in his lap and grins, pointedly ignoring my question. "You know the rules; we don't chat without something to occupy our mouths."

We sit in complete silence until Favier comes out with two glasses of bright red liquid. He sets one in front of either of us, bows, and leaves. "Thanks, Favier," I call after him. If the vampire hears me, he doesn't acknowledge it.

Magnus immediately takes a sip, moaning to himself the moment the blood touches his tongue. When he sets it down, he raises an eyebrow at me. "What? Is my stuff too good for you now?"

Reluctantly, I raise the glass to my lips. I take one sip, two, and the warm blood trickles down my throat. I set the glass back down, and stare blankly at my sire.

"You know," he begins, "I think you'd be great with Arabella. Truly. Forget the human; you'll only be held back."

No. Even if Gemma were to reject me completely, I'd never be able to be with anyone else. Least of all, *her*. "If this is all you want to talk to me about, I can go."

"It was worth a shot," he jeers with a grin. "I do want to talk about her, though. The human."

"Her name is *Gemma*," I say, my tone dripping with venom. "Not some human toy for you to dangle in front of my face."

"You have to admit, that has been pretty effective. More so than your precious little parents." He takes another sip from his glass. "Favier really outdid himself this time."

I resist the urge to push the glass away from me. I don't want anything from him, though this might be my only time to speak with Magnus, to negotiate with him for some sort of deal.

"What do you want?" I ask. "In order for her safety, what do you want?"

"For you to drop that tone with me, for one. I'm not your enemy, Quentin." He takes a deep breath and smiles, showing off his yellowed canines. "I'd like to offer her a place here, amongst us."

I freeze. I choose my next words carefully. "You want to turn her?"

"No, I want *you* to turn her. Then, the two of you can rule together. I get what I want; you get what you want. It's a win-win."

What I *want* is for her to choose me. She still hasn't made her mind up on if she wants to become an immortal, and I won't take that choice away from her. Besides, do I even want her as part of this world? She'd be much safer without me around at all.

Maybe I should just let her go.

"What do you want, then?" Magnus asks, slamming his fist onto the table. "I've brought you in under my wing, given you everything you've ever wanted. Now I offer you an eternity with your mate, and still, you turn me down? I feel like I'm being more than fair here, Quentin."

My defenses waiver for only a moment, but I catch myself. "I want to be free from you."

"Free? From *me?* Son, you can never escape my hold. I allowed you your little tantrum, but now it's time you come home. Don't you see? I *control* you."

No. I shake my head, trying to clear his voice from my thoughts. "No, you don't."

Magnus laughs, the sound echoing through the room. "You think that, huh?"

I stand from the table. "Our conversation is over."

"Like hell it is," Magnus says, sipping from his glass. "I'll see you around."

Personally, I'd like to rip his head from his shoulders, but I know there's no way I could do that and walk out of here alive.

CHAPTER 11
Gemma

My mind reels on what Quentin told me for the entirety of the following day. I have a late shift today, so the majority of the sunlight hours is spent hanging out alone at home. Micaela and Jayden both work, but I want to be left alone with my thoughts anyway.

He told me there's another vampire that both wants me dead and has a hold of him somehow. I don't know what to do. I only found out about vampires two days ago, and already, I'm being faced with this reality.

Should I pack and leave? Surely not; where would I go? Besides, I can't leave Micaela without a roommate, wondering where I am. And not being able to tell her the truth... it kills me. I just want to talk to her about it, see her perspective.

An idea goes off in my head. Why *can't* I tell her? It might take some convincing, especially without Quentin here to prove it, but Micaela told me yesterday not to keep any more secrets from her. This would be upholding that promise.

So, I pace around the apartment, waiting for her to come home. She works some sort of office job as a receptionist, but she loves the work. She's bubbly and loves taking phone calls and organizing things. It's perfect for her.

When I finally see her car pull into the parking lot through the window, my heart skips. What if she thinks I'm insane?

I don't have much time to fret about it, as before long, her keys are jiggling in the lock, and she enters the apartment. She tosses her keys into the bowl and starts to shed her boots, a tired look on her face.

"Long day?" I ask, lounging on the couch in what I hope is a very casual position.

"Yeah, three people called in sick, so I had to pick up some of the computer jobs. But it's nothing I haven't dealt with before. How was your day?"

My face turns grim, and her brows draw together. "I need you to sit down."

～

"So, you're telling me that Quentin is a vampire, and that's why you've been pining after him all this time?" Micaela asks. Surprisingly, she only called me crazy three times before finally accepting what I've been saying. She now sits across from me on the couch, legs crossed and sipping a glass of wine. She claimed she needed it to wrap her mind around this whole thing.

"I don't think him being a vampire has anything to do with my... obsession. He was certainly very human when we were kids."

"Let me see the bite mark again," she requests, and I push my hair out of the way. It's faded now, only two faded circular red dots instead of scabs. I have the feeling that it's not an ordinary type of wound, given how quickly it's healed. Micaela whistles.

"But what I really need to talk to you about is the whole his-vampire-boss-wants-me-dead deal. What should I do?"

"What *can* you do? If vampires can just disappear like that—"

"I don't think all vampires can do that," I tell her. "I think that's just a Quentin thing."

"*Either way,*" she says, glaring at me. "They're danger-ous, Gemma. What could you possibly do about it? You're quite literally their prey."

"I know," I say, exasperated. "But I can't just sit here and do nothing. I have to free him; I have to at least try."

"What would Quentin want you to do? Because I can assure you that it's not risking your neck for something he's trying to save you from."

"What would you do in my situation?"

"Well, for one, I'd break up with Jayden. You're still with him, right?"

That statement hits me hard. "Yeah, I'm still with him."

"It's not fair, Gemma. You've *kissed* Quentin. You had sex with him, for God's sake! Jayden deserves at least a clean break; you can't keep dragging him along."

I grip my hair. "I know! I know I'm being unfair, but I... I don't even know if I want what happened with Quentin to happen again. He's, well, he's *him*, but I love Jayden."

"Doesn't sound like you do," she says, and takes a long sip of her drink. "Look, you can do what you want, but I'm telling you, Jayden doesn't deserve how you're treating him."

She's right, of course. She's always freaking right.

There's a long few minutes of silence where I think hard about my options. "So, what *are* you going to do?" Micaela asks.

"I have to try and get him out of this," I tell her finally. "I have to try and free Quentin. I'm not sure how I'm going to do it, but I have to at least give it a shot. And then... I don't know what after that."

She nods, slowly. "Okay."

My head snaps up. "Okay?"

"Yes, *okay*," she says, downing the last of her drink. "I support you with whatever you want to do. No matter how absurd I think you're being."

I shuffle so I'm sitting next to her. I throw my arms around her, pulling her in tight. "Thank you, Micaela."

"Yeah, yeah," she says, but doesn't push me away. "Thanks for telling me *before* I find out for myself this time.

Even if you *did* wait a few days." Her eyes go wide. "Wait, is that what was behind all the commotion coming from your room last night?"

I pull away and rub the back of my neck. I chuckle slightly. "Yeah, nothing happened, though!"

She takes a deep breath and sighs, though there's a giant grin plastered on her face.

A buzzing fills the room, and I stand up. Jayden's here already, and I haven't even gotten ready for work.

"Go," Micaela says, gesturing with her hands at me. "I'll let him in."

"You won't say anything?" I plead. I already know the answer, but I have to ask.

"I won't say anything," she responds, rolling her eyes. "Now go!"

I bolt into my bedroom and quickly throw a couple outfits into my bag. It doesn't take me long to cover the marks on my neck, and then I throw a sweater on and shoulder my backpack before darting out into the living room.

Jayden's already here, standing with a wrapped box in his hand. His face lights up when he sees me, and I walk over and peck his cheek. "I got you something," he says, handing me the box.

"Yeah, and he wouldn't let me open it for you," Micaela says from the counter, shoveling leftover pasta into her mouth. "Alex hardly ever gets me presents."

"Thank you," I say to Jayden, ignoring my friend. "What's the occasion?"

"Just that I love you," he says. "Come on, you can open it in the car. I don't want you to be late."

I say goodbye to Micaela, and we head out to his car. I hold the present tight in my hands, trying to guess what he could have gotten me. A puppy is the first thing that comes to mind, but it's much too small and inanimate to be anything alive. On the other hand, the box is too big to be anything like jewelry.

When we slide into his car, I can't wait any longer. I open the present, and gasp when I see what's inside. "These spice jars are beautiful!"

"I remember you saying yesterday that you and Micaela don't cook often because you never have any seasoning. It's just a starter pack, but you've got pretty much all the basics there. Your parsley, cayenne, all that stuff."

I lean across the gap and peck him on the cheek. "Thank you."

"I can take it back to the house if you'd like," he suggests. "So, you don't have to carry them into work."

"I think I'll hang onto them for a while. All the girls are always showing off the gifts their boyfriends give them, and now it's my turn. Thank you, Jayden." I put the lid back onto the box and slide it into my bag. Luckily, there's enough room for it to fit.

As we continue the drive to my work, I'm even more conflicted now than before. Micaela was right; I don't deserve him. I've been horrible, terrible to him, and yet he's oblivious, bringing me gifts because I mentioned in passing that we don't have something.

I don't deserve him.

Outside, the sun begins to set. I know enough about vampires to know that the moment the sun disappears over the horizon, they're able to walk the streets with little identifiable features. My heart hammers in my chest at the thought. Even though I trust Quentin with all my heart, I don't know if any of the other vampires will spare me if it comes down to it, or if they'd just think of me as a meal.

When we finally arrive, I hop out and head toward the restaurant like I always do. And, like I always do, I wave to Jayden until he disappears down the street, and then a little more. Like every time I go to work, I duck my head and start walking straight for Temptation.

But this time, I don't make it there. I feel something large and heavy hit me on the back of my head, and every-thing goes black.

CHAPTER 12

Quentin

nstead of taking me back to that cell, Magnus lets me go back to my previous bedroom. It's large and extravagant, with red and gold decorations everywhere. I never added my own personal touches, though my clothes and knives are still in the armoire. This is all just another manipulation tactic by Magnus to pretend that everything is normal. It's infuriating.

I bet if I tried to walk out of here, he wouldn't even

stop me. He'd likely just have someone follow me, track my every move, and report back to him.

That gives me an idea.

I step out of my room, and though there are guards posted outside, they don't say anything. I nod to each of them in turn, but they don't say anything.

The maze of rooms and staircases is as familiar as the back of my hand. I used to spend days just wandering around, memorizing every corridor, every room and its purpose. So, it doesn't take me long to find the throne room. Luckily, Magnus isn't here. I'm not sure where he could be, but I slip through the front door without issue.

I'm honestly surprised I've made it this far. I thought for sure they'd stop me once I reached the throne room, the front door, or at least, the door to the sewer. But the man, Barth, even opens it and nods as I step out and into the tunnel.

I know the route to Gemma's house. It's engraved in my brain as sure as the layout of the underground mansion. But this time, I'm not going to give her a choice. I'm going to make it for her. I'll break her heart and tell her to go, and maybe, just *maybe*, she'll be safe. If she's out of the city and out of my life, she might still have a chance at a normal, happy life.

But when I get to the apartment, the first thing I notice is all the cop cars with their lights flashing, but no sirens. The next thing I see is the tape surrounding the front of the building. My stomach drops.

"Gemma?" I call out.

"Sir, we need you to leave," an officer says. Like hell I am. I prepare myself to melt into the shadows, dodge his questioning, and damn the consequences of using my power before a human, but I don't have to.

"Quentin?" It's Gemma's friend. I recognize her from the club. "Quentin, is that you?"

"Yeah," I say, eyeing the short, stout man in blue. "That's me."

"He's with me," she tells the officer. "It's okay."

"My partner will need to question him later," the man says at last, allowing me through. I duck under the tape, and Gemma's friend leads me into the building. I've never come through the front before, and it's odd standing in an elevator with her.

"Where is—" I start, but she presses a finger to her lips.

"Not yet," she tells me, and we continue riding up in silence.

She doesn't speak until we're inside the apartment, and she's closed and locked the doors.

"They've already done their search. Jayden was here earlier, but he had to go home."

"What's going on?" I demand. "Where's Gemma?"

She breaks down in tears. I've never dealt with someone crying before other than my mother and Gemma when we were kids, so I gently pat her on the back. "There, there," I say stiffly. "It's going to be okay..." I realize I don't know her name.

"Micaela," she says, wiping her tears. "Oh, God, here you are comforting me when you should be out looking for Gemma."

"Out looking for Gemma? What's going on?"

She sits down on the couch and gestures for me to do the same. "She didn't make it to work today. I'm her emergency contact, and they called me when she didn't clock in for her shift. But it was weird, because she left at the right time, and Jayden said she made it there fine—"

"Micaela," I say warningly. *Where's Gemma? Where's Gemma? Where's Gemma? Tell me she's fine; tell me she left the country because she's smart and knows that Magnus isn't someone to mess with.*

"Gemma's missing. We don't know where she is, and —" she cuts herself off, crying into her hands. "I wanted to call you and tell you what happened, but I don't have your number."

My entire world feels like it's in slow motion.

"How much do you know about who I am?" I ask, curious. How much does this human know about my world?

"Gemma told me everything. How you're a vampire, and there are people who want to hurt her to get to you. I— this doesn't have anything to do with that, does it?"

Probably. Absolutely. Maybe. Definitely.

"I don't know."

"She can't... she can't be *dead*, right?"

That statement snaps something within me. I stand up from the couch and go to leave, but then I stop. "Do you have anyone you can call and get to come over? For protection and for... consolation?"

She sniffles. "I can call Alex; he's my boyfriend."

I nod. "You do that. With all the police around, I doubt anyone will do anything, but... be careful, okay? I know Gemma cares about you."

Proud of the way I've handled this situation, I don't bother going to the door. Instead, I open the kitchen window and allow myself to become one with the darkness. My essence floats downward and onto the street, then I'm back to my full form.

Each step I take is precise, calculated. Each breath I take is a promise to Magnus that I will end him and every other vampire within his precious compound if he so much as lays a finger on her.

Back in the sewer, I don't bother with anything as mundane as a physical form. I only reappear once I've reached the sewer door.

"*Sanguis*," I say, but there's nothing. "Barth, open the door."

"They have your mate," comes his muffled reply. "I'm sorry."

I pound my fist on the heavy steel. "Open this goddamn door."

There's a creak, and then it swings open. Barth has a worried expression on his face, his brows drawn up and eyes filled with tears. "I have a mate. If anything happened to her..."

I nod in understanding. I don't know if Magnus has explicitly told him not to let me enter or not, but he must understand that I'd get inside somehow.

I nearly fly down the corridor. I can't bear to think about what has happened to her... if she's even still alive.

No. I know she's still alive. I'd know if she were dead; I'd feel it. Not only that, but Magnus knows that the moment she's dead, he won't have any power over me.

The moment I enter the throne room, my eyes land on her. Gemma. My Gemma, bound and gagged on the floor by Magnus' feet. Her eyes are wide and pleading, but I know it's not for her own life. She wants me to leave, but there's no chance of that.

Arabella is by her father's side, shooting daggers at me and looking like she wants to murder everyone in this room. Her fists are nearly shaking with it.

"What the hell do you want, Magnus?" I spit, continuing to walk up to the Lord.

"That's close enough, son." Magnus holds up a hand. I pause in my tracks, my eyes narrowing. "Your mate hasn't been bitten, and one more move will cause Arabella to slice her throat. Your choice."

My eyes roam over her entire body, checking for any sign of harm. In all, she looks okay, but terrified. I see red. I want to kill everyone in this room, to take Gemma with me and tell her it'll all be alright. But Arabella twirls her knife in her hand.

I think about using my powers, but the middle of this room has always been too bright for me to use them, anyway. I'm trapped.

"What do you want?" I repeat.

"I want your loyalty, Quentin."

"You got it," I say without question. "Let her go."

Gemma shakes her head furiously, the front wisps of her hair sticking to the sweat on her forehead.

"I'm afraid it's not quite that simple," Magnus says. "You'll need to prove yourself to me, of course. And then we'll talk."

My jaw clenches, and I ball my hands into fists. "You let her go now, and I'll be yours forever. That's my deal."

"The thing is," Magnus says, taking one step down and

closer to me. "I don't think you will be mine. Not truly, and certainly not so long as she lives."

"*You fucking touch her—*"

He holds up a hand. "You have a few choices. You can bite her and turn her now, if you'd like. Then, she'll be free to live here with you. Together, you could reign supreme." Arabella looks furious at this, but Magnus doesn't see his daughter's reaction and continues on. "*Or*, if you're so intent on keeping her a human — a cruel fate, in my opinion, to grow old and never truly experience life — you can prove yourself to me. Then, maybe in a couple years or so, I'll let her free. It's your choice, but either way, you're mine."

I curse at him, but Magnus simply laughs.

"I see you haven't yet made up your mind. I'll give you time to think about it. I'm not some horrible monster."

He gestures to a pair of vampires, who rush forward and grab Gemma by the arms, hauling her to her feet. "Careful," I snap at them. "Don't hurt her."

It's then when I notice that one of the vampires is Dante. The look he sends me... it's not his decision to have her here. At first, I'm angry, but then I'm relieved. At least I know Dante won't bring harm to my mate.

"You'll die for this," I tell Magnus. "You and anyone else who's involved."

Magnus leans forward, grinning widely. "Good luck."

CHAPTER 13

Gemma

As I'm led through the winding halls of the underground mansion, I find myself getting disoriented. It's a maze of winding corridors; the closer to the outside, the newer everything looks. It's almost as if they kept chiseling out and adding more rooms the more they expanded the grounds.

A brown-haired vampire leads me to my prison. He steps inside, the other vampire hanging back. The door clicks behind me, and I know I'm locked in. The bedroom is pleasant enough. Adorned and decorated in red and gold, it feels as if I were in a palace.

"I'm sorry," the vampire says, and I turn to face him. He looks nice, but I know looks can be deceiving.

"About what?"

"All this," he splays his arms wide for a moment, then they fall back to his sides. "I'm Quentin's friend, you know. I refused the order to go and kidnap you, so he gave me this." He lifts the hem of his shirt, and I gasp. A searing brand has been pressed into his skin, a large M with a circle around it. He lets the shirt drop. "He sent someone else to do the job, of course. I'm lucky he didn't kill me."

"How?" I ask, still staring at the place where the brand was.

He chuckles. "Fire still hurts us, even if we are immortal."

"Oh," I state dumbly.

He steps forward and juts out his hand. "My name's Dante, by the way." I take his hand and shake it, firm. His skin is cold, but not uncomfortably so.

"Gemma," I respond in turn.

He grins. "I know. Look, I have to go, but I'll be back in a little while to bring you some food." Before I can respond, he vanishes and reappears instantly in front of the door. I gasp. "Oh, right. I can teleport," he says and winks before opening the door and stepping through.

When my heart rate calms down, I explore the room I've been put into. It's grand, and nothing I would expect from a bunch of underground vampires. When I open the drawers, I see that there are clothes inside. When I pull them out, they look to be about my size.

"Are you okay?" Quentin's cool voice asks from behind me. I jump, squealing a bit. When I turn, I see him standing with his hands in his pockets. His body looks calm and collected, but his facial features betray that he is anything but. "Sorry, didn't mean to startle you."

"How did you get inside here?"

"Remember how I can melt into shadows?" I nod. "I become formless. I just slipped under the crack in the door."

"Magnus isn't... stopping you?"

"No," he says, stepping forward and brushing a strand of hair from my face. "This is likely his own form of torture. I can't take anyone else into the shadows with me, so he's dangling you in front of me. Reminding me that I'm powerless to save you."

"That's cruel," I say breathlessly. The closeness of our proximity is disorienting my brain. I can't think; I can't formulate educated sentences. "Why did they call me your mate?"

"Because that's what you are. Vampires are often... destined to be with someone. They can choose who, but once they pick — intentionally or not — no other will do." He bends down and gingerly, so delicately as if I'd break, kisses the corner of my mouth. "It's usually pretty obvious. But you didn't answer my first question."

"Hm?" My eyes flutter closed, and I wait for him to kiss me again. But he doesn't.

"Are you okay?"

I take a deep breath. It's a loaded question. "Physically? Yes. Am I happy about being kidnapped off the street? No."

Something occurs to me, though it isn't the first time it has. "Is—did...?"

"I spoke to Micaela," he assures me, placing his hands on my upper arms. "She'll be okay. She has Alex."

I nod, biting my lower lip. "I'll be okay, Quentin."

This seems to break him. He places his forehead to mine, and lets out a few shuddering breaths, halfway between a laugh and a sob. "I'm so sorry, Gemma. I didn't mean for this to happen."

"It's not your fault," I promise him.

"But it is. I'm the reason you're in this mess."

"You're *not*," I state firmly. "We're in this together."

We're both silent for a few moments, before he pulls away and takes a deep breath. "That's not why I came, though."

"You didn't come just to tease me and assure me everything will be okay?" I tease, my mouth quivering into a smirk.

"Not exactly. Do you know how to kill a vampire?"

Ah. This talk. "I mean, I've seen movies—"

"It's similar. There are two sure ways to kill a vampire: a stake through the heart, or direct exposure to the sun. Sun won't work here since we're underground, so you'll have to stake them. Decapitation works, too, but there's no way you'll be able to do that."

The seriousness of his words causes my eyes to prick. I nod eagerly, showing that I'm listening. "And fire. Fire hurts vampires."

He opens his mouth to agree, but then looks at me sideways. "How do you know?"

It occurs to me that Dante, although Quentin's friend,

might not have told him because he doesn't want him to worry. I shrug. "Dante told me. He was just trying to help."

He shakes his head. "Dante is a prick, but he's right." Quentin clears his throat, gesturing toward the various pieces of furniture around the room. "A table leg will work as a stake. Garlic only deters, so don't count on it to be useful. Besides, there's no garlic here, anyway."

That reminds me of something. "My bag! I had it on me when I came in. There was garlic powder inside. If you can get your hands on it, I can coat myself or something. Distract them for a moment or two while I can get the stake through."

His eyes glint with pride and... something else. "Gemma, you're a genius. Now, to actually use these things, you'll only have one shot, so wait for the perfect moment. Don't just take on your guards, as they'll just be replaced, and you'll be thrown into a cell. Pretend to be the doe-eyed damsel they think you are."

Pretending to be incompetent isn't exactly something I'm used to, but I nod regardless.

He walks over to me and embraces me in a hug. He kisses the top of my head. "I'm sorry, but I have to go. Magnus won't like it if I spend too much time here."

"Okay," I say against his chest, breathing in the scent of him. If it's the last time I'll be able to see him, I want to remember every detail.

I pull away, then stand on my tiptoes to plant a kiss solidly on his mouth. He's taken aback, but quickly recovers and kisses me back. I open my mouth to him as I've opened my heart and soul. My fingers find his hair, lightly tugging on the soft strands. His own hands find their way up the spine, against my skin and under the fabric of my shirt. My back arches against his touch.

"If I die... if I *die*, I don't want you to feel guilty about it," I mutter when we pull apart, gasping for breath. His hair is messy from my own doing, but I think it makes him look hotter.

"You're not going to die," he states firmly. He pecks my lips, but then he's gone. I'm left completely empty and bare. Utterly alone.

I take another look around the room, now examining for any pieces of furniture I could make into a stake. I eventually settle on the dresser, and pull it out from the wall so I have access to the back. Using my entire body and my feet as leverage, I manage to snap the back leg completely off the piece. I push it back into place against the wall, and check to make sure it's not immediately obvious that I've just vandalized the bedroom.

I snap off a few more small pieces to make sure the end is pointed, and shove it under my pillow. It's an obvious spot, but the easiest to get to in case I need it.

I lie on the bed for a while, watching the clock on the wall. It's early morning, which likely means that most of the vampires will be here, inside this compound, while the sun rises. I'm exhausted, not having slept all night, but when I try to lay my head down upon the pillow, my eyes won't shut.

"Food, as promised," a voice calls from the entrance. I sit up to see Dante, dressed in a similar outfit to Quentin, but much simpler and a brown-gray top. He reaches into his pocket and pulls out a little jar about three inches in height. "Oh, yeah, here. Quentin told me to give you this. I risked my neck getting it to you, but I can see how it would be useful."

"Thanks," I say, and accept the dish and garlic powder with genuine gratitude. I slip the jar under my pillow alongside the stake. It's from the spice kit Jayden got me.

Jayden. I've spent so much time thinking about Micaela and how she must be feeling, but I haven't given my boyfriend much thought. What does that say about me? Guilt shoots through me, and I look down at the warm bowl in my hands.

It's soup, but thankfully, chicken noodle and not tomato. I don't know if I could stomach anything red right now.

He stands there while I eat the first spoonful. "How is it?"

"Fine," I respond plainly. "Why?"

He rubs the back of his neck and sits down at the edge of the bed. "None of us have had real food since we turned. We can't keep it down."

So, that means Quentin has consumed nothing but blood for *years*? "Oh."

"Also, I made it from a can, so I was just wondering."

The spoon clinks against the bowl as I take another bite. "Why don't you just taste it and spit it out?"

"That's an awful waste," he says, his nose turning up in disgust. "Besides, it would taste like ash, anyway. Our taste buds are heightened to blood by some primal instinct."

And I've just lost my appetite. I place the spoon in the bowl and look at him properly. "So... teleportation, huh?"

His eyes light up. "Yep. I can only go places I can actually see, so no teleporting through doors or outside the building or anything, but it's helpful in a fight."

"Why doesn't everyone fight against Magnus? Everyone I've seen so far looks miserable."

He takes a few heartbeats to answer. "He can be very... persuasive. You know how he captured you to control Quentin? He's done the same to virtually every other vampire who doesn't agree with what he says. Most just accept him as the leader because they have nowhere else to go; society won't accept them purely because they're... us."

So, he has someone that Magnus is holding over his head. That means that his help and assistance will only go so far. "I'm sorry."

He changes the topic. "Quentin loves you, you know. He'll do anything to get you out of here."

"That's what I'm afraid of."

Dante shoots me a small, sad smile. "Same, Gemma. Same."

Aweek has passed with Gemma stuck up in that room, and I've yet to get a clear answer from Magnus. It's all been "patience, son" or "prove yourself first."

All I've been doing is dirty work. The jobs that even the lowest clan members refuse to do. Missions such as the *pick-up* job Dante and I did together. I didn't once complain, but I wasn't happy about it, either.

So, when that seventh day comes, I'm furious.

My boots pound against the floorboards as I march down the hallways. Others jump out of my way to avoid my wrath, but I'm not focused on them. I briefly stall when I near Gemma's door, but continue on toward my goal.

Magnus, I know, is in his throne room. I throw the door open, and I see him speaking with a sobbing woman kneeling on the floor. Arabella is beside her father, and both their heads turn to me.

"You're dismissed, Clara," Magnus says dismissively to the woman at the base of throne. "Think about what I said."

She nods and quickly darts off. I've never seen her before, but I don't care.

"What is it going to take?" I snap, walking up to the throne and pausing at the base. "What the hell is it going to take to get you to let Gemma go?"

Magnus takes a deep breath and lets it out slowly. He opens his mouth to respond, but I hold up my finger.

"And don't you *dare* give me the same bullshit answer you have been for the past week. Tell me what I have to do, and I'll do it."

"Something a little beyond begrudging compliance would be a start," Magnus tells me with a smirk. I glare and wait for him to continue. "I'm not seeing true devotion from you, Quentin."

"What more can I do?!"

"Kill your parents." He says this so plainly that I blink in surprise, allowing myself to process his words.

"Kill my—"

"I know they mean everything to you. Kill them, and I'll let Gemma go under the guise that you stay here. But I'll have to send her off somewhere you'll never be able to follow."

"How will I know she's alive then?"

"Proof of life will be provided upon request. I think that's more than reasonable."

I don't know what to say. I'd do anything for Gemma, absolutely *anything*, but *this*? Killing my own parents?

"Take your time; think about it. After all, I myself am perfectly fine if you want her to stay locked up for the rest of her life. You can visit her whenever you'd like, but she'll have to stay here. Of course, she'll soon grow old and die, so I'd make your decision rather quickly." He grins, and then raises a finger in the air. He waves it back and forth. "Tick tock."

I storm out of the throne room. I don't realize right away, but I've exited through the main doors to the sewer. Someone chases after me, and I recognize the footfalls as belonging to Arabella. My blood boils, and I continue walking, but she grabs my shoulder.

"What?" I snap, coming to a halt and spinning around to face her.

She raises a delicately arched eyebrow. With a purr, she says, "My offer is still on the table. We belong together, Quentin. I know it; my father knows it. Why can't you see it?"

I shake with rage. "You're foolish."

"Tactless perhaps, but not foolish. We're likely the most powerful vampires of our age. A union would be most profitable."

"I have a *mate*," I snarl. "What makes you think I want *you*?" She flinches, but I continue. "Besides, if you're so worried about the perfect union, go marry Dante."

Her nose wrinkles. "He's too... tamed."

I let out a singular, humorless laugh. "So, you only like me because you think I'm some sort of wild beast? Is it the chase that gets you on? Seriously, Arabella, I didn't think you were so shallow."

Her face becomes hard, and she backs up a few steps. "Go fuck yourself."

"Right back at you." I make my way down the hall once more, and this time, she doesn't follow.

In my blind rage, I almost don't notice that it isn't Barth at the post near the sewer door.

I don't know where I intend to go, but somewhere away from the vampires is a start. Somewhere away from Magnus and his goons that has had me ensnared since the moment I turned.

Kill my parents; save Gemma. Be under Magnus' thrall for the rest of my immortal existence. I don't exactly see a mutually beneficial answer here.

The streets are quiet. There's a sort of chill dew hanging in the air, even though it's not currently raining. I can smell the muted scent of decay, and know autumn is on its way.

I don't bother with my mask. What's the point? There's no way I could go back to my previous life. No way I could live amongst humans once all this is over. It was foolish to hope, anyway.

The park is nearly empty. I used to come here often at

night and sit on the benches. I hardly remember what it was like to sit under the sun with dozens of other people and the congregating sounds of cars and nature. A life spent in the darkness, and an eternity more to go.

As I come closer to the park, I notice there's one man sitting on one of the benches. Whatever, there are usually quite a few homeless people who spend the night on these benches. They're decently comfortable, and so long as the police don't catch them in the morning, they remain relatively undisturbed.

Unfortunately, the homeless are the primary targets that Magnus sends his vampires out to get. During my time away, I warned a few of them, advising them like I did Gemma on how to kill one... or at least, protect themselves. I'm not sure if anyone heard or even acknowledged my explanations, but it was worth a shot.

As I come nearer, I find that the man on the bench is sobbing. He's dressed in a suit, though his hair is disheveled. Still, I'd recognize him anywhere.

Jayden. Gemma's human competition and a secondary reason behind my rage.

I find myself sitting next to him. He looks up, startled. "Oh, sorry." He wipes the tears from his eyes. "I—I thought this park was empty."

"What's wrong?" The words are mine, and yet they sound so foreign. They feel so... human.

"Ah, not your problem. I'll be alright."

"If there's anything I know, it's that crying doesn't make someone alright."

Jayden takes a deep breath and gives me a sheepish grin. "My girlfriend is missing. She has been for a week. I just got the news today that they're placing the case on hold. There haven't been any new leads; it's as if she just vanished into thin air."

My first emotion is vague agreement. The vampires Magnus has trained are highly capable, and there wouldn't be so much as a fingerprint left at the scene. The second emotion, however, is rage. How could the police just stop looking for someone? Do they not know that this woman has friends? She has people who love her, people who depend on her.

"I'm really sorry," I say finally.

"Not your fault," he mutters, and a pang of guilt shoots through me. It *is* my fault. It's entirely my fault.

"Still, I'm sorry that's happened to you. Are you going to give up searching?"

He looks at me as if I've just stated the most absurd thing on the planet. "No! Absolutely not. The police are completely overlooking a witness just because he was under the influence. He said he saw two cloaked men dragging a girl into an abandoned building just off Main Street."

Another tactic. While one pair takes the real victim underground, other pairs act out dragging a vampire of similar height and build all around the city. I myself have been part of this diversion before. "Don't give up," I tell him. "She'll turn up one day."

"I hope so. I was going to propose to her, you know? Gemma's great, and my family loves her. I—I don't know what I'd do without her."

I don't know what to say. Jealousy, this emotion I'm feeling is jealousy. That Gemma has the chance at a normal, boring life with this man. Where they can go out in public, get married, and even have kids if she wants. With me, none of that is possible.

I find myself feeling terrible for this man. He doesn't deserve any of this; least of all, my interference in his love life. I can almost see why Gemma likes him. He's stable, and he cares. He's not rotten or a monster like I am.

He stands up and brushes off his pants, looking slightly embarrassed. "Thanks for listening, but I should go home. Just in case she tries to call, you know?"

I nod and stand up myself. I'm quite a few inches taller than him, but he doesn't look at me again. He simply walks off into the night, shoulders hunched and dragging his feet with each step.

Gemma deserves him. Not me, but *him*. She should be able to experience that proposal and spend the rest of her glorious human years by his side. She's having a hard time deciding between the two of us, so I'll make it simple for her and remove myself from the equation.

I have to go kill my parents, but first, I have to say goodbye.

"Ha, I win!" I exclaim, standing up and doing a little happy dance around the room.

Dante grumbles and resets the board, placing the chess pieces back in their designated spots. "Beginner's luck," he mumbles.

I stick my tongue out. "You've been saying that for days now. Just admit that you suck at chess, and I'm the best at it!"

Dante and I have gotten to know each other well over

the past week, since I haven't once been allowed outside my cell. There's an adjoining bathroom, and I have all my meals delivered to me. Apart from that, a woman comes around once every few days to tidy up and take all my clothes to be washed. If I wasn't being held against my will, I'd think this might be fun. Quentin doesn't come by often, as Dante tells me he's being sent on mission after mission, and being watched like a hawk. It's not easy, but at least I have this goofy vampire to keep me company.

"Go again?" Dante asks, setting himself up as white and making the first move. I slide back into my chair opposite him, and think for a moment before moving my piece.

We go back and forth a couple more times, and on my next turn, I smirk. "You really didn't see that?"

"See wha—oh, no!" He waves his hands frantically, going to move back the piece he just moved.

I click my tongue and move my queen up, taking the pawn right in front of his king. "Check*mate*."

"I can't believe you got me in four moves," he groans, tugging on his hair. An idea goes off in his brain. "Why don't we play Connect Four or something?"

"If you want to go get the game, be my guest."

"Alright fine, I'll play *one* round—"

The door bursts open, cutting him off. Both our heads swivel around, and a tall, beautiful woman walks in with fire in her eyes. She looks prepared to kill, and based on how her eyes are fixated, I'd say her target would be me.

I stand up, Dante following suit. "Arabella," he starts, but she silences him with a look. She pauses a few feet away from me, looking my figure up and down with a plain look of disgust. I cross my arms and allow her to finish.

"You look so goddamn fragile. How did *you* manage to capture him, huh?"

"Who?" I ask flatly. "Quentin?"

"Of *course*, Quentin! Who else would I be talking about?"

She has a point. "Look, I didn't *capture* Quentin. All I want is to go home. I have a boyfriend."

This doesn't seem to comfort her. She laughs, the sound both lovely and condescending. "Oh, great! Not only has he turned me down for a *human*, but he's turned me down for a human who doesn't even reciprocate his feelings. How quaint."

I seethe. "Don't call me a 'human' like that."

She leans closer. "I'll call you whatever I want."

"Arabella, cut it out," Dante interjects, teleporting himself between us and raising his hands to her. "You know what Quentin will do if he finds out you're threatening her."

"Out of the way, imp. So far, I've only insulted her, with no promise on the end of her life. If I wanted to threaten her, I'd tell her I'll tear her apart, limb from limb, and let her bleed out as she writhes, unable to do anything but watch while I drink her blood. *That's* a threat."

I gulp. It certainly *is* a threat. I take a step back.

"Quentin would burn down the manor, and you know it," Dante says softly, as if he were reasoning with a child. Based on her anger, I'd say she's been acting like one.

"She doesn't even *want* him." She peers over Dante's shoulder to meet my eyes. Every muscle in my body screams to look away, to avert my eyes and bow in submission. But I stand tall, matching her intense glare. "Why are you here, human? Why couldn't you just leave him alone?"

"I don't know," I answer honestly. It's the most honest I've been with myself in a while. As much as I love Jayden… the fiery passion I experience around Quentin can't be matched. It's as if Quentin represents the person that I want to be, and Jayden is the person I need to be.

The question is, who do I desire more?

By now, some of the guards in the hallway have heard the yelling and come to check it out. Arabella looks around and, seeing that she can't do much more, decides on spitting at the ground near my feet and stomping off and out of the bedroom. The guards hang around for a few more minutes before dispersing back into the hallway. Soon, it's just Dante and I remaining once more.

"How eventful," he comments, and sits back down on the chair. "Where were we?"

"Gemma." It's Quentin's voice; I'd recognize it anywhere.

"Ah, man," Dante mutters under his breath, and teleports to the door. He winks at me before he leaves, acting out a vulgar gesture and pointing at Quentin's figure on the other side of the room. I laugh.

"What, are you two friends now?" he asks. He's in a mood; I can tell. But even so, he puts on a smile and comes over to kiss me.

"We've become close," I admit. "What's it to you?"

"He's a prick," he utters while planting his lips to my forehead.

"You've said that before, but I just don't see it."

He hums and pulls away slightly. "Look, I wanted to say goodbye."

"What? Are they setting me free?" I can feel my spirit lift. I'll be able to go home and see Micaela again? I can finally get out of this suffocatingly luxurious prison?

"I have to do something first, but then... yes. You'll be free to go."

"There's a catch," I say, placing my hands on my hips. "There's always a catch."

"Let me worry about that part," he tells me, pulling me toward him with one arm and brushing my hair to the side with another. He kisses me square on the mouth, and my knees wobble at the touch.

"Quentin," I mumble against his mouth. "What's going on?"

He sighs, but pulls away. "Please, just let me do this, and you can go on with your life. Everything will be okay."

I shake my head violently. "No."

"Jayden loves you. You two can live your lives together—"

"No!" I say again, staring him in the eye. "You don't get to make that decision for me."

"It's the only way—"

"It's *not* the only way. Whatever you're about to do, it's not the only way. I refuse to believe that." My breathing deepens, and my hands are shaking at my sides. "You can't let him win, Quentin."

He gives me a sad smile and reaches out a hand to cup my face. I lean into his touch, and he caresses my lips with his thumb. "I don't deserve you," he mutters more to himself than to me.

When he goes to take his hand away, I grab his wrist and hold it in place. "We deserve each other. Please, Quentin. Don't do this."

He opens his mouth to speak, but he doesn't get the chance. Dante bursts inside, face twisted in terror. Both Quentin and I look at him expectantly, wondering what the problem is.

"Magnus wants to see Gemma for dinner. He thinks you're out doing *it*, Quentin."

"What?" Quentin and I both ask at the same time, though in vastly different tones. I look over at him, and he's standing unnaturally still.

"What does he want with her?" Quentin asks, his words careful and direct.

Dante shrugs, shaking his head. "I don't know. I was told to bring her down to the dining hall."

I look at Quentin, who looks lost. "I'll go. You stay in the shadows outside the room. If anything happens, you'll be right there. Just don't let yourself be seen." He nods, and I stand on my toes to kiss him on the cheek. "I'll be okay."

"Come on," Dante says impatiently, checking the clock on the wall. "He doesn't like to be kept waiting."

I go to step away, but Quentin's hand reaches out and grabs my wrist. "I don't like this," he states firmly. "I don't want you anywhere near that man."

"I know," I say, and he loosens his grip. With a last thought, I rush over to my bed and pull out the jar of garlic powder. I give them both a nod, and slip it into the space between my breasts. I check the mirror and ensure that nothing looks out of place. I leave the stake behind, as there's nowhere I'd convincingly be able to hide it.

Without another word, I follow Dante out and into the hall.

It's the first time I've been outside the room in a week, and I'm reminded of just how large this mansion is. Winding corridors with no real structural layout, I wouldn't be surprised if there were hundreds of secret passages I'd never know about.

How many times has Quentin walked these same hallways, not as a prisoner, but as the heir? This was his home for so many years, and it's just a shame that the leader of it all is a raging psychopath.

The dining hall is larger than I imagined it would be. A gigantic cavern cut into the rock, it looks like it could seat hundreds. Two long tables line each side, and a singular raised one runs parallel at the head. Magnus is already there, with his hardened face and blood-red lips. His hair, as always, is styled perfectly atop his head. If I didn't know who he was — *what* he was, I would assume he didn't know how to fight at all.

Dante finds his place near one of the pillars and stands, stone-faced and unmoving. Quentin, I know, is somewhere close. I suspect he won't be able to blend into the shadows for long, so he wouldn't be able to be inside this room, but certainly within shouting distance.

I sit down at the table opposite Magnus, my back to the hallway I just walked down.

"Gemma," he says, stretching out each syllable. "Thank you for joining me."

He snaps his fingers, and a man rushes over. He's a vampire, but obviously not as high up as Magnus or the others I've seen. He places a tall silver goblet before Magnus and a plate before me. I look down, and my mouth waters at the sight of roasted potatoes, chicken, and green vegetables.

"Eat," Magnus instructs, gesturing toward the plate dramatically. "You've been surviving on canned food; you must be starving."

I am. I pick up the fork that was provided beside the plate, and stab into the beans first. It tastes so *good*. I love Dante for bringing me the — sometimes cold — soups, but this is just so much better.

Magnus takes a sip from the goblet, and I know, without seeing the red ichor left on his lips, that the cup contains blood.

"I could offer you sanctuary," he mentions after a long minute spent in silence, with him watching me eat as if it were the most fascinating thing on the planet. "You could become a vampire, take over my throne with Quentin once I step down. It's relatively painless — the process. I believe that's the only way everyone will win."

I pause with my fork halfway to my mouth. "You'd let me... rule?"

"Of course. You're Quentin's mate, and an incredibly strong-willed human. I can't imagine how powerful you'd be if you were an immortal. And besides, you could have a power! They're never revealed until you're turned, so just imagine the possibilities." His fingers drum against the table, and there's a sly smile upon his face.

He makes sense. I'd give up my humanity, and I'd be able to live alongside Quentin for the rest of eternity. If I stay human while Quentin lives forever, eventually I'll grow old and die. At some point, he'll be left with nothing. How is any of that fair?

I find myself nodding slowly, wanting to agree with everything he says—

I want to agree. Magnus *makes* me want to agree. But the truth is, I've never wanted immortality or even a boring life with Jayden; I've only ever wanted Quentin.

"Manipulation." I breathe. From the corner of my eye, I see Dante take a step forward. "Your power is manipulation."

The smile disappears from his face. "Excuse me?"

I raise my chin a little higher. "All this," I splay my arms out wide, "is because you've manipulated every single vampire into doing your bidding. Not just through threatening their family or offering them a home, but because they can't resist you, can they? You say something, and they're compelled to do as you say. Am I wrong?"

For the first time since I first laid eyes on this man, his expression is murderous. He stands up in his chair. "Why you—"

I reach between my breasts and pull out the garlic powder shaker. I take the lid off, and toss the contents onto his face. He reels back, screaming and brushing it off his face. I take the opportunity to stand and start backing toward the door. But Magnus is quicker, and jumps over the table with ease. A wooden dagger finds its way into his hand, and he pulls it back over his shoulder. Human or vampire, a stake through the heart is a sure way to perish.

But a body slams into me that wasn't there moments before. A scream finds its way past my lips, and the wood finds its place in the exact spot I was standing.

Dante collapses to the ground. I try to catch him, but his body is too heavy for me to hold. We tumble backwards, and I feel more than I hear the gasps of his breaths. He's still alive; thank God, he's still alive. If I can get him somewhere, they could save him.

"Tell Quentin I'm sorry," he whispers, his words barely more than the movements of his mouth.

And then he's gone. The essence that once made Dante who he was, is entirely gone.

CHAPTER 16

Quentin

When I hear Gemma scream, everything in my body shudders with it. I should have never left her alone with that man. I *knew* something would go wrong.

I burst through the doors, not bothering with my powers. I want Magnus to see my face, to know it's me.

He's standing before Gemma and Dante, both of whom are lying on the ground. Gemma's crying, and there's too much blood on the ground for it to be anything but death. My eyes meet my former master's, and he goes stiff. He bolts out one of the back doors, and a murderous rage consumes me.

"Quentin," Gemma whimpers, and all my attention goes to her. Dante is dead, a wooden knife sticking out from the left side of his chest. "He said... oh, *God*. He said he's sorry."

Sorry for what? But there isn't time to question or deliberate on a dead man's words when we have to get out of here. I run over and grab her arm. "Come on, Gemma. We have to go."

"I can't leave him," she says, her face covered in tears, and her body shaking as she cradles his head on her lap. "We can't just leave him here."

"We're all going to be dead if we don't go," I tell her. If I know Magnus as well as I think I do, he's already rallying forces to kill both of us and cover everything up.

"He can manipulate," she says through her sobs as she reluctantly stands and steps away from Dante' body.

"Yes, I know. He's really good at that. Now, let's *go*."

"No," she says. "You don't understand. His power— Magnus' *power* is manipulation. The others can't help but follow him."

My mind reels with this information, trying to find a scrap of evidence that it's false. I can't. I let out a long string of curses.

"I mean, it makes sense, doesn't it? Why hasn't anyone rallied against him in such a long time?" She spares a glance at Dante. "You managed it, but that's because you were directly opposed to what he was saying."

One of the side doors bursts open, and in comes a stream of vampire guards. "We have to go."

"I see that," she snaps. I pull her along to the exit, but along the way, grab a chair and throw it to the ground. I pick up as many pieces as I can before continuing to run along to the exit.

When we slip out into the hallway, I pull aside a tapestry and push her inside. It's a small hole that's barely used, but I've known about it for years. It's the same place I hid in while she dined with that bastard. I place my hand to her mouth to keep her from saying anything as the guards rush past, their shadows flying across the inside of the tapestry from the lanterns in the hallway. I'm hyper aware of the closeness of our bodies, her warmth filling the alcove.

When I'm sure they're gone, I release my one hand and examine the stakes in the other.

"When I disappear into the darkness, any inanimate object I'm holding goes, too," I explain. "Some vampires might not know yet what's happened, but a human walking down the hall with stakes in her hand is sure to arouse suspicion."

"What are you saying?" she whispers. I hate the way her voice quivers with fear. I hate the way she had to watch one of her friends die in front of her. I hate how she's covered in a vampire's blood already, and in the heart of a building with people designed to kill her.

"You'll have to sneak down the corridors. Don't worry, I'll be right there in shadow form giving you directions and making sure the way is clear. Can you do this?"

She lifts her hand to wipe the tears from her face, but all she does is smear blood under her eyes. I lift my thumbs and gently wipe her cheeks. I then lower my mouth to hers and kiss her, hard. If it's the last time we ever get to hold each other, I want to memorize the way her mouth moves against mine. I want to memorize the way she buries her hands into my hair and pulls me close. I want to memorize it all, even if it comes to the grave with me.

"Let's go," I whisper into her ear, and before she can plant her lips against mine again, I disappear into the shadows. My consciousness shoots down each side of the corridor, and I check for guards or other vampires that might pose a threat. Down the left side are some of the guards, deliberating on where we could have gone. I rush back to Gemma. "Right," I whisper in her ear. I watch as she shivers, but hops down from the alcove and starts walking down the right corridor.

For about five minutes I do this, telling her to go right or left based on which way I think is the safest and will bring us closer to the front door. I'd like to avoid the throne room as much as possible, but there is a way that takes us to a door right beside the one that leads to the exit. So, all she'll have to do is open the one and slip into the other right next to it.

"Left," I say, and she pivots on her heel. "Keep your gait even," I remind her for the third time. "Walk too fast, and you'll attract attention. Too slow, and we won't make it anywhere. We have to—"

"I know!" she snaps, cutting off my rant. I have the feeling that if I were a physical entity, I would have gotten slapped.

Guards erupt down the hall, and I hear their footsteps. They haven't noticed Gemma yet, but I make the quick decision to tell her to jump into the room on her left. She does, and what I see is even worse.

Arabella, standing with two of her closest friends, lounging on a couch. I mentally smack myself. I should have checked the room first; this is certainly worse than facing the guards outside.

I'm about to tell Gemma to just turn around and leave, when she straightens her spine and shouts at Arabella, "You know, it never made sense why you stuck by your father even though he treats you like dirt. Now it does."

Oh, Gemma.

"Excuse me?" she asks, standing. Her two friends follow suit.

"You didn't know your father's power is to manipulate those he speaks to? Well, that's quite a shame, honestly. Thought you must have known, especially since you follow him around like the—"

My body falls into a solid form, and I throw an arm in front of my mate, stopping Arabella in her tracks. I tuck the hand with the stakes behind my back and hope they don't see them.

"*Quentin*," she spits. "What poisoned lie have you been spreading to this human about our father?"

"So," Gemma says snidely from behind me. "You want to marry him, but you consider him your brother? That's sick."

"You wouldn't know, *human*. All vampires are brothers and sisters in arms. Magnus is a father to us all."

"That sounds like a cult," she states boldly. "But listen, I'm telling the truth. None of you have free will here. Haven't any of you ever thought of *why* you decided to come? Perhaps it came to you one night after a long spell of not talking to Magnus? Only for all your doubts to go away the moment he told you that this is what you want, that this life is what you need?"

If there's any way I could love her more, I do in this moment.

Arabella's two lackeys, girls I've never met before, share a glance between each other. Arabella's eyes just narrow, and her nostrils flare with every breath.

"She has a point, Bella," the blonde-haired girl meekly states. Magnus' daughter swivels around and points at her lackey's chest.

"No, she *doesn't*. Magnus is the only reason we're not hunted and killed by humans. He's the only reason we can live without fear—"

I tune her out, nudging Gemma back with my arm. She must have gotten the hint, because she takes a few casual steps back until her fingers touch the doorknob. Then, she opens it slightly and slips out and back into the hallway.

She lets out a deep breath. "That was close," she says, but I simply disappear.

"Right," I mutter, close to her ear. I watch as she shivers, her eyes trailing all around, but never actually landing on where my consciousness is.

She turns around the right corner, but I don't let myself feel hopeful. We're so, *so* close now. Just a few more turns, and we'll be free.

"That door on your left," I tell her. She grasps the doorknob and pulls it open. The throne room is dark, which is a good sign that Magnus isn't in here. "The door is on your right to the tunnel."

But the moment her fingertips brush the doorknob, the one behind us slams shut, and the room illuminates in bright, white light. The same that could be found inside the cell they kept me in the first time.

My body forcefully comes into full physicality, the stakes clattering to the floor with the shock of it. I hear Gemma rattle the door. It's locked.

Two sets of hands reach out and grab my arms, and I look across the room to see Magnus. There's a set of guards at each door, though they're now coming into the middle to protect their leader.

"A great design of this manor is that nobody can enter or leave without first paying tribute to their Lord. I'll give it to you; I didn't expect either of you to make it this far. And yet here you both are." He's so smug, *too* smug. I wish I could pound his face in and be done with it.

I look over at Gemma. She's not being restrained, which is a big mistake. Magnus may not think much about humans, but my mate is special. She'll figure a way out of this.

His eyes flash from the fallen stakes, to me, to finally landing on Gemma. "I'm surprised with you, girl. I certainly didn't expect you of all people to figure out my little secret. What gave me away?" His stupid grin. His stupid, stupid grin on his even more so face.

"I was agreeing to something I didn't want to," she states as if it were obvious. "I wouldn't have done that without some sort of magical influence."

He hums to himself and crosses his arms over his chest. "Well, you see, the great thing about my power is that it works on anyone, whether they're aware or not. In fact, since you're aware, I don't have to worry about subtlety." He snaps his fingers, and the guards pull me away, farther from Gemma and the stakes. "I've made arthritic humans dance. I've forced complete strangers to give up their deepest, darkest secrets. I've made vampires kill their loved ones."

Magnus looks at me and smirks. Boiling hot rage floods through my entire body, and I think I'm about to burst with it. I struggle against the vampires holding me, but their grip only tightens.

"So, Gemma," he says finally, looking at my mate. She looks so fragile, so small now. I have to protect her; I *need* to protect—

"Kill Quentin."

No.

Gemma goes rigid. I think she's fighting it, fighting Magnus' command, but she bends over and picks up one of the stakes from the ground. She turns toward me, her face completely blank and void of any emotion.

"Gemma," I plead, but she doesn't so much as hesitate. Her entire body is focused on raising that stake above her head and stepping closer to me. "Gemma, I love you."

No, no, no. This will ruin her; it'll *destroy* her.

From somewhere else in the room, Magnus laughs. He's clearly enjoying this show. "Go on, Gemma. Bury that stake in Quentin's chest."

Though to me the words sound normal, absurd, I've been on the receiving end enough times to know what it feels like. Even if I didn't know it at the time, Magnus' words are so powerful and enchanting. It's like everything else fades away, and there's only him and the sounds he feeds into the brain.

She's standing so close now, her face immovable. She's perfect, even like this. I resist the urge to close my eyes.

Then, the corner of her mouth twitches, and she spins. So fast for even an immortal's eyes, her already-poised arm snaps forward and sends the spike of wood soaring through the air. It lands home, straight into Magnus' chest.

He staggers backward, gasping. He glances from the stake to Gemma, eyes wide with terror. "How—"

He's dead before he hits the floor. One thing I almost forgot about Gemma is how much she loved javelin as a teenager.

The hands holding my arms slacken, and I take the opportunity to shake them off. I don't bother trying the doorknob. I kick the entire thing open with the heel of my boot. The wooden door splinters and swings open on the hinges, Gemma already running down it.

She slows down for a moment, and I pass her. She grabs one of the lanterns off the wall and smashes it on the floor. It lights, causing the carpet in that area to light up in hot, burning flames. She takes off back down the hall, overtaking me once more.

The light from the throne room has seeped into the hallway, but the moment the shadows return, I slip into them and shoot past her. I land just in time to send my fist into the doorman's jaw. He falls to the ground, unconscious.

My hands find the latch to the porthole, and I lift it.

"Hurry!" Gemma says, looking back down the hallway to see the vampire guards rushing toward us.

The door swings open, and she jumps out and into the sewer. I follow suit, slamming the door shut behind us and pulling her into the nearest side-tunnel.

We walk along the stone pathways, and I search above to find an appropriate porthole for us to climb out of. After I think we've made enough turns to at least slow down our pursuers, I find one that looks relatively easy for her to climb. I hop onto the ladder and push open the grate. I climb out myself, then reach out my hand to help her up.

She disregards my help, and climbs up the ladder in no time. I slide the hole back in place, and when I behold our surroundings, I curse.

"The sun," she breathes. "It's rising."

Indeed, it is. The golden rays are starting to peek over the horizon and cast a glow over the town. I grab her arm, and we take off down the sidewalk. A few people stop and stare, others shout at us.

The first rays of sunlight find their way over a building, and I hiss when my hand passes through one of the beams of light.

"Put your hood up," she demands, and I do so. I flick the hood of my cloak up and over my head, concealing my head, at least. But still, it won't be good if I'm still out when the sun is in full effect.

Gemma takes over leading, and she ducks by different streets. Our shoes hit the pavement in synchronizing rhythms.

"Hey, you two!" someone shouts. It's a cop, and he's pointing at the two of us. Notably Gemma, with blood all over her shirt and hands. "Stop!"

We keep going. The police officer chases after us, but I

make the split-second decision to vanish and reappear next to him, using my elbow to slam into the back of his head and sending him sprawling out onto the sidewalk. I rush back to Gemma's side, and place my hand on her back. "Come on," I whisper. "Let's go."

"You go to the apartment; I'll meet you there," she tells me, her breathing becoming ragged.

"No way I'm leaving you," I respond and pick her up over my shoulder. She protests, but only for a moment. I can move just as fast while carrying her, and even faster than when I was trying to slow my pace to match hers.

Finally, her apartment building appears in our view. I skip the front lobby, and opt for climbing the fire escape instead.

I adjust my hold on Gemma so she's on my back, and she throws her arms around my neck. I climb up with relative ease and spare a glance to the sun. It's climbing... and fast. It gets to the point where my hands start to blister and burn under the ultraviolet light, but I don't slow in my ascent. I can't.

We make it to the window of her bedroom, and I don't bother knocking. I place my palms against the glass and heave it open, snapping the locks on it that attempt to prevent the exact thing that I'm doing.

I push Gemma inside first, then climb in myself. I pull the window back down, but it no longer closes all the way. I'll figure out a way to make it up to her and her landlord.

She turns to face me, a large grin on her face. It's an eerie sight, considering she's covered in Dante's blood. Dante...

"We did it," she says, breathlessly. "We actually did it."

"Yeah," I respond, smiling and pulling her to me. "We did."

I plant my mouth on hers.

The bedroom door creaks open, and it's Micaela's voice that demands, "Quentin, you know we have a front door, right? And Gemma, is that *blood*?"

Epilogue

GEMMA

"You're certain you want to do this?" Quentin asks for the umpteenth time that night. "I mean, it's a big step—"

I silence him with a kiss.

We're currently standing at the edge of the park, and it's evening. We're tucked under an old oak tree, and Quentin is wearing his cloak. I made him wear black leather gloves along with it, so I don't have to deal with more blisters on his otherwise perfect skin. He complained about it, but agreed when I told him he'd have to apply the soothing ointment to his own skin.

"There he is," Quentin jeers. Before I can turn around to see, he vanishes into the shadows. I sigh, but turn around to see Jayden walking across the park. I wave to him, and he waves back, quickening his pace.

"I can't believe you're okay," he slurs, throwing his arms around me in a bone-crushing hug. "What happened? You didn't explain much during our phone call."

"My dad showed up, and I was terrified, so I went into hiding. I'm so sorry I didn't tell you. I was so caught up with past feelings that I didn't really think. He's gone now, and nothing happened, thankfully."

He nods, pulling away to take me in. "You look good."

"I'm really sorry I scared everyone; it wasn't my intention. I sometimes forget how much I mean to people." I feel awful about lying to him, but what am I supposed to say? That vampires kidnapped me, but I killed their leader so everything's fine? Or try to make up a story about some kidnappers? This is the most realistic answer, and closed the police case after some brief questioning. They believed me easily due to an obvious lack of wounds and evidence to prove otherwise.

"Well, next time, just send me a text, okay? I was worried sick!"

"Look, Jayden…," I start. "I had a lot to think about while I was away." I didn't realize this would be as hard as it is. I take a deep breath and think about Quentin. I'm doing this because I love *him*, and Jayden was never supposed to be my forever.

"Yes?"

"I'm sorry, but I have to break things off. I'm going to move north, see where things take me." There, it's out. The truth, even if it's only half of it.

"Is this about your father?" he asks without hesitation. "Are you worried he'll come back?"

"Yes and no. I just realized that I'm not living the life I really want. I hope you understand."

There's a pregnant pause where I can tell he wants to say something, but struggles to find the right words. He looks hurt; he looks absolutely devastated. But at the same time, understanding flashes over his features.

"I'm just glad you're alright," he reveals finally. His tone sounds completely genuine, which furthers just how horrible I was to him. "And I hope you find happiness."

"I hope you do, too," I add, wrapping my arms around him for one last hug.

We say our goodbyes, and soon, Jayden leaves, and I know I'll never see him again. Quentin waits a minute after Jayden leaves before revealing himself.

"No going back now."

"What do we do about Arabella? The other vampires? Surely, they'll be after us, looking for revenge." The panic comes to me all at once. "Quentin, they'll hunt us."

"All the more reason to move far, far away. We'll change our identities, find a small little house together somewhere in the north. I've already made arrangements for my parents to move, and you warned Micaela against staying here. There's nothing more we can do." He brushes a strand of hair from my eyes. "Besides, they'll be too busy fighting each other and picking up the pieces to do anything until we've settled somewhere nice and cozy, just the two of us."

"I think I'll like that," I tell him, grabbing his hand in mine. "Just us two. No distance or crazy father figures."

"Just the two of us," he echoes. "From now until the end."

MORTAL MATE

VIOLA TEMPEST

www.ingramcontent.com/pod-product-compliance
Lightning Source LLC
Chambersburg PA
CBHW031026190726
48286CB00003BA/1040